Winterland

A Dark Fairy Tale

by Mike Duran

8/8/2018
R.L.S.

Winterland
A Dark Fairy Tale
By Mike Duran

Cover design by Merrie Destefano.
Cover image by ©iStockPhoto/gioadventures.

CONTENTS

Winterland: A Dark Fairy Tale

ONE

A snowflake struck her windshield and dissolved, leaving only a watery, wind-driven, smudge. Had she been in Maine or British Columbia, Eunice Ames would have thought nothing of it. But summer in Southern California was not the place for random snowflakes. So she took her eyes off the road and squinted at the liquid streak evaporating on the glass.

As she did this, a man bolted from the shadow of the overpass into the path of her late model Audi station wagon. And she hit him.

His body disappeared under the vehicle and the onyx crystal hanging from the rear-view mirror struck the windshield on impact. The crystal did not shatter. However, in that split second, all that mattered was that Eunice slammed on her brakes.

Which turned into a skid and the skid turned into a chain reaction.

The Audi jolted to a stop. Her seatbelt tightened and she pitched against the restraint. If the car had airbags, she was sure they'd have deployed. Instead, the vehicle came to rest cockeyed in the slow lane.

A car swept past with its horn blaring. Then another.

But Eunice's mind was fixed on the man under her Audi. What was he thinking? Why'd he been running onto the freeway? Was he dead?

Thump! Da-dmp! Several concussions reverberated behind her.

Eunice sat with her heart in her throat as the peel of tires and the crunch of metal sounded. A rush hour pileup of epic proportions was now unfolding. Sound and smoke and the blur of motion exploded around her. She gripped the steering wheel, preparing to be catapulted into eternity.

Yet Eunice Ames remained earthbound.

In the next lane, shards of rubber exploded and a skin of tire slapped the asphalt. Horns blasted amidst low-level thuds. Someone cursed. Two lanes over, a passenger car swerved just in time to miss another that had fishtailed to face the opposite direction. As the entire freeway ground to a stop, a bank of grey noxious smoke drifted over Eunice's car, gliding across the asphalt like fog on a bayou.

And the crystal twirled wildly over the dash.

As it did, Eunice could not help but think about its significance. According to her mother, onyx helped one achieve emotional balance and build self-confidence. Mother was up on her onyx and convinced that her daughter required such *alternative* assistance. Of course, Eunice thought it was all a bunch of hooey and told her mother so. But now with a tumor strangling her mother's brainstem, Eunice had called a truce and took the crystal begrudgingly, as an olive branch, hanging it on the rear-view mirror as testament to her concession. Besides, it looked cool. And at the moment, she could use all the emotional balance and cool-points possible.

Expecting the door to be jammed, Eunice leaned her shoulder into it and pushed. It popped open without resistance. She unbuckled her seatbelt, slung her legs out of the Audi, and sat there trembling, unprepared to take the next step. There was no blood on the pavement, but that didn't quell her fears. He was under her car and probably dead. Or dismembered. Or both.

Her heartbeat reverberated through her limbs like aftershocks from a SoCal temblor. Drawing the back of her hand across her forehead, she realized her flesh was clammy. Was this the early stages of shock? Or maybe the prelude to unconsciousness. The lights from the twirling crystal only added to her anxiety, so she reached over and snapped it from the mirror.

Eunice stepped out and stood wobbling with her hand on the open door.

"Hey!" someone shouted from behind her. "Hey, lady!"

But she was too woozy to bother looking.

A whiff of radiator fluid struck her like smelling salts. She cupped her hand over her nose and turned to see the freeway stacked behind her, cars strewn haphazardly, a compressed metallic river of ghost flames and rising exhaust. A baby cried somewhere. A man in dress slacks and a vest paced the tarmac nearby growling into a cell phone, and a stereo rumbled unseen causing windows to reverberate. A single stream of automobiles crept along the fast lane, and with each passing, a new face emerged, pasted to the glass, hoping to catch a glimpse of the jerk who'd jacked up drive time.

Eunice drew a deep breath, stepped away from the station wagon, and bent sideways at the waist to see who was underneath. Yet from where she stood, there was nothing—no blood, no body parts, and no body. Could he have gotten up and ran away? Had the impact sent him flying? Come to think of it, had there even been an impact?

Eunice glanced into the sky, just to make sure there were no snow clouds.

"What is it?" A tall, olive-skinned man in business attire approached from the opposite side of the vehicle. He surveyed her front bumper before squinting skeptically at Eunice. "D'ya hit something?"

"My mother's dying," she blurted.

The man skidded to a stop. "Huh?"

"Brain cancer. She… " Eunice swallowed dryly. "I was on my way to Saint Luke's. They called me. She's… she won't make it through the night."

The man stared at her, then said, "I'm sorry."

"And that guy," Eunice continued. "He… *Didn't you see him?*"

Now the man was gaping at her.

Behind the Audi, a white Lexus sat aslant, inches from her hatch. In the drivers' seat, a dark woman with gaudy sequined sunglasses chomped gum and strummed her nails atop the steering wheel.

"He came from over there." Eunice pointed, trying to compose herself. But her hand trembled as if she was going through withdrawals again, so she quickly returned it to her side. "Just ran out. I wasn't watching—I mean... It happened so fast. I barely had time to stop."

She took a step back, trying again to locate the body, but the motion made her dizzy

"I didn't see him," the man confessed, continuing his approach. He stopped and stood studying her. "Listen, are you okay?"

Eunice reached up and massaged the nape of her neck. "I'm alright," she said unconvincingly. He glanced at the fist that she had gripped around the crystal and raised one eyebrow. She quickly shoved the smooth, two-inch stone into the front, right pocket of her jeans and looked sheepishly at him. "Really, I am."

"Okay," he drawled. "Then where's—?"

"I dunno. He was..." She stooped forward, hoping not to disrupt her now fragile equilibrium, and gazed under her vehicle. "He was right around..."

The man walked to the front of the Audi, hoisted up his pant legs, and squatted down. Gripping the fender, he leaned over and peered underneath it. Then he rose, shaking his head. Eunice grimaced and prepared for the worst.

"There's nothing here." He put his hands on his hips and looked quizzically at her. "What the hell happened?"

Behind him, an oblong sun, stained orange-brown by the L.A. smog, stretched wide along the western skyline. Except for rogue cars escaping from the fast lane, the westbound 210 was empty. The vast concrete landscape silhouetted the Lexus man, as did the brume sunset, transforming him into a cardboard cutout against a movie screen. A drug-induced mirage could not have looked more surreal. Then, as Eunice stood staring at the man, the panorama behind him seemed to flutter—a slow-rolling spatial distortion that swept across her field of vision like a ripple on the surface of a glassy pool.

Eunice swayed front to back.

"Lady? Lady, you all right?"

The man had stepped close enough for her to smell aloe and cologne. He extended his hand and said something else, but his words were now inaudible. In fact, everything was on mute—the cursing, the honking, the idling engines, the whirlybird overhead with its camera trained on the commotion—all drowned out by an unfolding anomaly.

Eunice stood enthralled, hallucinating maybe, for just beyond this man, space appeared to be moving.

She squeezed her eyes shut and lightly touched her temples with her fingertips. The stress had finally caught up to her. What with her mother dying, the anxious commutes to and from the hospital, and their perpetually tenuous relationship, Eunice had finally hit the wall.

Either that or a decade's worth of narcotics was catching up to her.

Drawing a deep breath, Eunice opened her eyes and refocused. But despite her stellar demonstration of resolve, the atmosphere behind the Lexus man rippled again.

Her jaw grew slack and any composure she'd mustered dawdled down her spine and evaporated into spongy knees.

The man motioned her to sit back down in the car. But she stood mesmerized because just beyond the Audi hung what appeared to be a translucent veil, an atmospheric sheet that swayed like a curtain on a stage in the wake of someone's passage.

Her mother often proclaimed that metaphysical phenomenon had its roots in science—a rare concession to rationality on her mother's part. Multiple dimensions were no longer the exclusive realm of shamans and psychonauts. Now even the geek in the lab coat questioned the nature of reality.

Of course, her mother used that argument to reel Eunice in, to keep her off-balance. But at the moment, Eunice was just off-balance enough to risk validating this phenomenon.

She brushed away the man, unconcerned about appearing rude, and stepped toward the shimmering invisible curtain.

And that step—whether one of faith or foolishness—made the strange barrier come alive. For the farther she walked away from her car, from the Lexus man, from the angry knot of commuters, and into that elusive field, the more it began to snow.

TWO

It was a glistening veil, a translucent shroud that undulated as she approached.

But unlike Alice's rabbit hole and Narnia's wardrobe, Eunice's dimensional curtain opened to a world strangely similar to her own. If a threshold had been crossed, she couldn't say exactly when or where, only that things had changed. And were changing with every step. For the worse.

She glanced up into the powdery, snowy diffusion, and then leveled her gaze ahead. The empty freeway still stretched toward the western skyline, but both the freeway and the skyline were growing gray, becoming sepia replicas of themselves, a dreary world of ash and bone. She peered forward as the tarmac yielded to roots and oily scabs. The overpass glistened with a sheer vegetative skin. Her steps slowed, but it was wonder, not fear, that provoked the deliberation. Was she imagining all this? Or was it the flip side of the freeway, some type of parallel plane into Dante's inferno? If James Cameron was looking for a location for his next Terminator film, Eunice had just discovered it.

The chatter of the circling helicopter melded with another sound, a discordant moan or beacon in the distance. Instead of a vast swath of empty concrete, the road now lay strewn with indistinct mounds of debris, the dividers choked by weird black brambles. It had stopped snowing, but pockets of dirty melting ice remained. Dark clouds lolled overhead like pirate masts on a languid sea. The highway now spilled into a basin of burnt orange. Crumbling overpasses marked the path of the road, before disappearing into a swamp of distant haze. Smog billowed above this murky plain like massive thunderheads, and a hole opened in the horizon where the sun used to be. Engines of steam churned within this ozone gash, an angry vortex ringed with ash and fire that sent dark columns roiling skyward.

She always knew L.A. was a hellhole.

"… don't know… pale lady… ambulance…"

Eunice stopped at the sound but did not turn around. A faint glow framed the periphery of her gaze, as if the morning sun shone at her back. By all estimates, she had advanced only several yards from her vehicle. Now she felt leagues away. The snow had turned to soot. It swirled at her feet and the ashen sun belched fiery strands into the skyline. Were she to retrace her steps, Eunice knew she would leave that otherworld and return to the exhaust, the anxiety, and the Lexus man who wanted her to sit down.

"… ccident… neck… ay… ith…"

Couldn't he see she was having an epiphany? No, of course not. He did not know her mother was dying from cancer or that a fiery portal had punctured the world. And she wasn't about to tell him.

"… id… ahl… unt... to…"

She closed her eyes again. Maybe she had hit her head during the accident, died and passed into limbo. Or somewhere worse. Occasionally, people came back from death with a new lease on life. Perhaps this was that. Of course, she'd already made her peace with God. But standing in that bleak, charred otherworld, Eunice wondered if she should reevaluate her spiritual state.

"She wants you."

The voice was not that of the Lexus man. Eunice opened her eyes to see dark clouds fomenting overhead. She had moved in deeper, somehow, without actually moving. A red pall now tainted the landscape and the beacon had become a shrill cry peeling in the distance.

"She wants you."

A figure standing nearby came into focus. She took a step forward and reached toward him. "You're the guy—! Are you alright?"

"More or less."

"But I hit you."

"Uh, not exactly."

He was a young man, boyish really, with fair features. His head seemed slightly misshapen, sunken on one side and the eyelid there drooped a little, but was bright. The man/boy stood crooked, tilting left like a fixture in a house of gravity.

"Am I...? Where am I?" she asked. "And what is that?" She motioned to the burning place on the skyline.

"It's the end of the road. That's where she is."

"*She?*"

"Your mother. Or what's left of her. Her Coronation is beginning."

"My mother?" Eunice squinted at the bent man. "But she's in a coma."

"Her body is. But souls have a way of—how can I put it—*migrating*. Just look at you."

Eunice glanced at her body to make sure it was still there. She brushed off several dirty snowflakes. Then she shook her head in stupefaction. "Okay. I'm gonna need a minute here."

"It's your minute. But, just so you know, the clock's ticking on this thing."

"Now what do you mean by that?"

He jabbed his thumb toward the broiling crimson skyline. "Why do you think she called you? She's running out of time." He paused for a moment. "And you saw me."

Eunice gaped at the young man. Part of her wanted to play along with him and see where this was going. But another part of her—the cautious, analytical, suffocatingly boring side—was weighing in with red flags and fire alarms. If she conceded to this surreal reality, she might go mad. Crazy people were crazy precisely because they believed in alternate worlds where the souls of their dying relatives watched. Yet even if running was the rational thing to do, she couldn't see returning to the hellacious traffic jam she had caused. At least, not just yet.

"So what is this place?" Eunice asked.

"This is the way she came—once, a long time ago." He looked up into the black ocean overhead. "It's a mess, I know. It's changed a lot. Always does." He shrugged dismissively. "Anyway, if you don't do something, she'll get stuck here. Become the Queen." Then he leveled his gaze upon Eunice. "And, trust me, that'll be bad."

The elasticity returned to her knees and she wavered.

Chronic meth addicts sometimes experienced *amphetamine psychosis*. You don't extract the demons from your veins without a fight. Hallucinations were customary in the battle—or so she'd heard. Mr. Q, in rehab, had heated discussions with a garden gnome he named Julius before, one day, decapitating it with a shovel. The drugs had siphoned his sanity. Shortly thereafter, Mr. Q. was carted off, never to be seen again. Was that her fate, to become a babbling halfwit lost in some dream state on the 210 freeway? And just one week after graduating and returning to the "real world."

She closed her eyes again, hoping, praying, for a lifeline. And as she did, the distant wail rose, shrill, swelling ever louder.

It was a siren beckoning from the other side.

"You can go if you want."

Eunice opened her eyes and looked sideways at the crooked man. Then she turned to see cars—or at least, what were once cars—piled behind her like dunes on a beach, melded together, rolling away into static and white foam. The air between here and there seemed to shimmer with kinetic vibrancy. She remained peering through this atmospheric curtain as the siren approached with its gauzy red lights pulsating, wove its way through the car dunes, and neared the two of them. She shook her head in incomprehension.

"Don't worry, you can go back," said the man reassuringly. "It's not that far away. It never is."

The siren grew closer.

"... spit... get... ff..."

Eunice shook her head faster, as if trying to rattle something free. "But... my mother. She wants me."

"Oh well, that's the way it goes. Life's full of consequences. We turn to; we turn away—can't do one and not the other. We jump, we fall. We fall, we come here. I didn't make the rules, Eunice."

She winced as the siren came closer.

"...er... down lady..."

She swung toward the bent man/boy and studied him. He looked tangible, real, unlike a dimensional veil or a garden gnome. In fact, he appeared humored by her scrutiny and stepped closer to accommodate.

"May I?" she asked.

"So you're staying?"

"Don't know."

He shrugged. "Sure."

She tapped his shoulder, cautiously at first, and then squeezed his bicep, as one would test a loaf of bread. Then Eunice took a step back, her eyes pinched with puzzlement. "Who are you? And where the heck am I?"

"I'm Joseph. And this—" he nodded toward the savage highway and the flaming orb on the horizon, "It's her world— the wreckage or, better yet, the *ripening* of everything she's chosen. And for whatever reason, you've been granted access."

His words were so matter-of-fact, so void of guile and deceit that her disbelief deflated. A terrible alignment was happening, an awakening that Eunice dare not stop. She turned and looked again at the black hole sun. It was bigger than before, a monstrous globe radiating molten spires, bathing the world in its crimson fury. The vision, in its enormity, seemed to swallow the siren and the babbling Lexus man. In their place rose the sounds of desolation, the low moan of wind sweeping across the blighted afterworld.

Eunice faced the boy with a chilling sense that she had not lost it, that something far more than a hallucination or flashback had encroached upon her.

"Joseph."

"Yes."

"What do you want?" she said. "Tell me again."

"Me? I'm just a trekker, a tweener. It's her, your mom. She's the one who called you."

"And she wants…"

"She wants you to free her, Eunice. You know, gather loose ends, cut ties. All the stuff that people do when they, you know… when the end is near."

Eunice peered at him, but the brightness of his bad eye had not dimmed. His words rang with the same unnerving honesty.

"Free her. Maybe I can heal her of cancer while I'm at it," she said in mock bemusement. "Listen, I've got enough problems of my own and I'm supposed to… *free her?* How?"

"Well, for starters, by *conceding*."

"Concede. Right." She nodded blankly. "And what, exactly, am I conceding?"

"Everything." Joseph opened his arms wide. "Conceding to this. And to that." He pointed to the wound in the sky. "And to fight."

Fight. The word made her spine stiffen. Yeah, she knew about fighting. It's what she'd spent the last three years doing. Fighting the lies, the fear, the self-loathing, the compliance to generations of dysfunction and addiction, the infernal hunger that seethed in her genes. Always teetering near complete disintegration and ruin, she had clung to hope. If Eunice Ames could do anything, she could fight.

Staring into that surreal borderland, she said, "You're going with me, right?"

"Absolutely."

"And I can go back whenever I want?"

"Yup."

Eunice nodded. "Concede, huh?" Then she turned to him. "Okay, Joseph. Then lead the way."

Without a word, he turned and began limping toward the boiling horizon. She watched him for a moment and thought about the world behind her, on the other side of the weird dimensional doorway—the world of sirens and Lexus men, the world of cancer and crystals and drug addicts losing their jobs and their families, shivering in alleys and under overpasses where they would inevitably die alone; the world of broken dreams and bitterness, where mothers sell their souls and fathers are nowhere to be found.

"Free her," she said to herself. "Lord knows she needs it." And with that, Eunice caught up and followed Joseph along the blasted highway, into that ominous inner world. She did not look back, or want to, for a very long time.

THREE

Joseph's pace was unhurried, but swift. He swung his leg as he walked, a motion that reminded Eunice of an odd dance step. She watched him out of the corner of her eye, trying to grasp where she was and trusting that his proximity would somehow tether her to sanity. But their descent toward the fiery vortex had tweaked her equilibrium and become an exercise in perspective.

Everything seemed to radiate from the volcanic sun, as if it were a womb and the highway itself was the afterbirth of some hideous cataclysm. But just how far away it was, Eunice could not ascertain. At once it looked both near and distant, an immense mirage in the atmosphere that fluctuated with the slightest of ones' motions. Ghost flames swirled off the tarmac, complicating the view, and shadows jittered along the landscape like spastic marionettes. Her eyes stung from the parched air, but she remained fixated, curious, and not a little skeptical.

As if he were intuiting her thoughts, Joseph said, "There's no getting used to it. Things change here, and depending on where she's at, they can change pretty drastically. So don't try to figure it out all at once. The stuff you really need to know, you'll learn along the way. But the important thing is that we keep moving."

Eunice nodded to herself, but his words did nothing to satisfy her growing perplexity. *It's her world*, Joseph had said. *The wreckage, the ripening of everything she's chosen.* Eunice could easily imagine her mother's interior life looking something like this—dark and blasted and inhospitable. But how had Eunice gotten here, and where exactly was she— inside her mother's thoughts, inside her mother's soul? Or was this some type of psychographic arena where scores were settled? Either way, Eunice would have a hard time explaining this to her support group.

They hiked under a collapsed overpass, zigzagging through rubble and twisted rebar. Angry vines choked the pillars and drifts of ash clung to their base. High above the crumbled arches, a vortex had started churning in the clouds, as if someone had pulled a plug and the stormy ocean was being drained into the sky. Nearby, a green freeway sign lay crumpled. Despite gouges and rust wounds, she could make out the word *Winterland* on it. Eunice had commuted the 210 freeway through Pasadena for years, but she had never seen an exit named Winterland.

"Joseph," she finally said. "How do I know this place is real?"

He glanced at her, and kept plowing forward without a response.

"Maybe I bumped my head back there," she mused, "got a concussion or something, and now I'm... I'm delusional." She jabbed her finger into the air. "That's it, huh? I'm suffering from shock."

Joseph shook his head. "I thought we already covered this."

"This *is* a hallucination, isn't it? Or some type of flashback. I'm still on the freeway—the cars, the Lexus guy—they're still right here. But this—" she motioned to the apocalyptic landscape. Then tapped her temple with her forefinger. "It's all inside my head."

Joseph clucked his tongue and looked away.

"I bumped my head," Eunice continued, "and now I've got this journey to complete. Something to resolve. But it's all psychological. My mother's dying and I've got some personal issues to work out. And this is, like, the subconscious manifestation of that. Kind of a catharsis where I battle my demons, forgive my Mom, and resolve to go on living without her. Mm-hmm. Now I get it."

If her imaginary adventure failed, Eunice was suddenly convinced she might have a career in psychotherapy.

Yet Joseph seemed unimpressed with her reasoning. He continued limping down the highway. Eunice watched him, hoping for a reply, some confirmation of her muddled thesis.

Finally, he said, "Do you always over-think things?"

Eunice wrung her brow, feeling slightly offended.

"Look," she said. "I'm just trying to make sense of this. It's not every day that you get in a car accident and then... and then this snowy *space* opens up in front of you and, and this guy that no one else can see, he—*wait a second!* You're the one who started this! You ran out in front of my car. This is all your fault."

"Hey, you're the only one who saw me. So whose fault is that? Besides, you agreed to come."

"Well, yeah. But the least you could do is cut me some slack."

"Okay. Just don't over-think things. That's all I'm saying. Around here, that can be dangerous."

She knew about the danger of over-thinking things, becoming fixated upon an idea or emotion to the point of collapse. In fact, the very suggestion sent her mind wheeling. It was symptomatic of meth users. The brain couldn't run that high without risking a complete flameout. She'd heard the same story, over and over. An addict was going along just fine, a thought was triggered, and suddenly everything snowballed. The next thing the person knew was they hadn't eaten for three days, they'd picked every scab on their body raw, and they were an emotional wreck Madness was not the result of not thinking, she came to believe, but thinking too much.

In fact, as Eunice pondered this, she caught herself gnawing her fingernails. Once again. It was a disgusting habit.

Joseph looked at her and scowled.

She brought her hand to her side and felt a flush of shame.

After a moment, Joseph said, "Eunice, have you ever thought that she might be right?"

"Who?"

"Your mother. Do you think the only reality is the one you can see?"

"Well, no. But—"

She scrunched her lips and surveyed the barren landscape. It sure looked real enough. The ground under her feet was solid, her eyes and nostrils stung from the acrid air, and Joseph's body cast a shadow across the ground. If this were an hallucination, she'd have a hard time disproving it.

"So…" Eunice said cautiously, "let's say I'm not delusional. This is really her world. And this quest—it has real consequences. Let's just say all that's true. I'm still gonna need some help."

"That's why I'm here." He half-bowed.

"Okay. So where we're going—tell me again—what am I supposed to do?"

He appeared to be mulling the question. Finally, he shrugged. "Free her."

"Right," Eunice drawled. "But she's dying—at least, back *there* she was dying."

"Oh, she's dying here, too. Only, it's a different kind of death. A second death, you could say. When she dies, night falls, and her world will stop changing. It'll crystallize. She'll be crowned queen. And when that happens, no one can save her. She will be enthroned forever."

"So…" Eunice struggled to make sense of his words. "How am I supposed to change that?"

"That depends on where your mother's at. Could involve a game of wits, maybe even bloodsport."

"Bloodsport? Against who? I'm not killing anyone!"

"Or any*thing*?" Joseph lingered on the word, as if to draw out its implications. "Each person's different. I'm not sure what's in her world. All I know is that you need to reach her. Because if you don't, she'll be stuck."

Eunice squinted, and looked sideways at Joseph. "So is this—" she had to force the word out, "*hell*?"

"Well, it isn't Kansas."

She scowled at Joseph, taken aback by his bad humor as much as its implications.

"Sorry," he said. "That sign we passed back there. Remember?"

"You mean the one that said Winterland?"

"Yeah. You don't remember seeing that sign before, do you?"

"Not on the 210. But we're not on the 210. Are we?"

"Sort of. Now that you're here, you've brought your own reality—which should brighten things up considerably."

"Is that a compliment?"

"You can take it as one. Anyway, by the looks of it, I'm guessing you came this way a lot."

"The 210? That's an understatement. We lived in San Fernando, and then Pasadena, both off the 210. And then I got a delivery job serving that whole corridor. I practically lived on the freeway."

"Well," said Joseph. "Then that explains it. You're partly seeing what you're used to seeing. Only this freeway— your mother's—is populated by her: her regrets and beliefs, her inner voices and imaginary friends; the things she's let grow. Which explains the sign."

"I'm getting a headache."

"Druids and Wiccans believed that when they died, their souls went to a place called *Summerland*."

"Okay, Mom," Eunice said sarcastically.

"They referred to Summerland as *The Land of Eternal Summer*."

She laughed aloud. "Well this is hardly a land of eternal summer." Then she suddenly understood, and said somberly, "Which is why she named this place Winterland."

"Exactly. If Summerland was a land of bliss and heavenly delights—"

"Then Winterland would look like a highway to hell."

Joseph nodded. "Now you're catching on."

They crossed over some skid marks and sidestepped a pool of oil. Further on, a length of guardrail dangled from its post and they crunched over a field of shattered glass. So was Eunice making this up? Did this glass and oil—did this very freeway—even exist? Or was it simply a part of her mother's fading reality? Despite Joseph's efforts to enlighten her, she felt as confused as ever. And having mentioned that word again...

"Joseph," she finally asked. "Then is this hell?"

"Let me put it this way—it's *becoming* hell. A very personal kind of hell. Right now it's kind of a crossroad, an intersection between eternities. What it becomes, in the end, is up to us. I mean, you can't water weeds your whole life and expect to harvest roses. Well, this is the eternity your mother's watered."

She stopped and put her hand on his shoulder—it was as tangible as the first time she'd touched it. He turned and they stood looking at each other.

"Joseph? My mom doesn't believe in hell."

He snorted, "That doesn't mean it isn't real!"

The low moan had become a distant wail, an omnipresent air-raid siren on an endless loop. Eunice listened to its lonesome bay echoing across that wasteland and pondered his words. She had reached the end of her rope a long time ago with her mother, and traded in their religious debates for civility and tolerance. Besides, hell was for serial killers, pedophiles, and preachers that swindled money from little old ladies, not for aging hippies who attended séances and environmental rallies.

Nevertheless, there she was, in this infernal Oz, commissioned to free her mother from a place the woman didn't believe existed. And all the logic in the world couldn't seem to change any of that.

Maybe Joseph was correct—she should stop trying to over-think everything.

"You're right," Eunice said to herself. "That doesn't mean it isn't real."

As she spoke the words, a stench drifted by that yanked her gut into her throat. It may have been the most awful stink Eunice had ever encountered, an odor more akin to toxic contamination than anything. She flung her arm over her face, barely able to keep from vomiting. But behind the noxious smell, something loomed; a presence more vile than anything Eunice had ever encountered.

FOUR

Eunice doubled over dry-retching. The smell was so bad the air seemed to thicken with its rottenness. Gulping back the rising nausea, she turned toward the skyline, in the direction of the awful smell.

A massive twisted object now lolled on the highway just ahead of them, perhaps three stories high, black and brooding. Root-like tentacles grappled for traction like some long-dormant subterranean beast rising from the asphalt plane.

If she hadn't been in shock before, she was now.

"That part about not over-thinking things," Eunice stood gaping. "I think this is it."

"We gotta hurry!" Joseph began marching straight for the colossal form. "C'mon!"

But Eunice stayed put. Where had this thing come from? Only moments before, the highway had been barren. She stayed with her hand over her nose, watching Joseph limp toward the tangled monstrosity.

Suddenly, he turned back and yelled, "You said you'd fight. Now come on!"

The exhortation burrowed into her mind like an ornery splinter. *Fight.* Yeah, she had conceded to fight. Yet this was not playing out how she expected. What exactly was she supposed to be fighting here? If it came down to sheer willpower, Eunice might have a chance. But by the looks of things, this battle might involve physical dexterity. And if that was the case, she had about as much chance as Tinkerbell versus Megatron.

She remained with her hand cupped over her nose, contemplating the immense beckoning shape. Then she sucked air through her teeth, set her face toward the awful black menagerie, and lurched forward. And the moment she took that step, the mysterious object crystallized in her vision.

"A tree!" she exclaimed. "It's a tree."

"That's it," Joseph shouted over his shoulder. "A tree! That's always the first thing."

But this was unlike any tree she had ever seen. It lay across the highway like a dying sea serpent, mangled limbs sagging earthward, cancerous digits spread in appeal to a waterless sky. Oily sores marred the tree's flesh and withered translucent sacks dangled from its leafless branches like foul ornaments. Its roots had caused a great upheaval, leaving the highway cloven with gaps and buckled concrete. The earth was charred and blasted there, as if nuked into infertility. And the stench—

She hurried to Joseph's side, unable to look away from the decrepit thing. "What kind of tree is this?"

"Not a healthy one, that's for sure."

"Can't we go around?"

"You can never get around it. Not in a hundred years. You'd just keep goin' in circles. Besides, there's someone waiting."

"A person?! Here?"

But Joseph kept slogging forward.

The odor became more oppressive as they went, a gaseous haze rising from the earth and blanketing the area in a thin noxious veil. Eunice gagged. "Joseph, please!"

"If you stop, you'll lose her. I'm telling you—you will never wanna come back. No one does. When they see the truth of it, no one ever wants to come back."

She pulled her shirt up over her nose and, afraid to get too near the pestilent tree, angled her way toward the periphery of its branches. Splattered fruit had stained the ground under its umbrella, leaving a demented abstraction on the blackened earth. The spilled juices had flowed together in spots and turned to tributaries forming a single black stream that sludged its way into the distant basin. Only then, under that baneful canopy, did Eunice realize the aura of death that clung to that place. Something malignant grew there, something so diseased that the very earth was tainted by its sickness.

Joseph and Eunice navigated knuckles of roots and crumbling concrete until the tree's branches became a tangle atop them, a skeletal frame weighted with the wretched pods. She began to worry that one of the poisonous fruits would drop on them and, as they picked their way across the terrain, she kept glancing anxiously overhead.

"C'mon!" Joseph stood on the opposite side of a gnarled root. "Don't slow down." Then he added, "And don't think about it!"

She glowered at him.

Suddenly a commotion sounded above and brittle limbs exploded, showering the area. Eunice threw her arms over her head to protect herself, but not before glimpsing strange forms—humanoid, winged creatures with tiny round heads and long legs, skating into the eventide. Twigs clattered to the ground around her. Yet at the moment, Eunice was not worried about getting clubbed by an errant limb. There were others here—things not human.

Up to that point, her journey had been more like a fantastical experiment or a test of wills. Heck, if she was free to go back whenever she pleased, what real risk was involved? Yet under the shadow of this death tree, it seemed like the stakes were changing. This adventure was no longer about catharsis or subconscious play-acting. It was about survival.

"Hey!" she shouted to Joseph. "You said I can go back. Right?"

He poked his head from behind a moldering fallen branch. "We just started."

"Yeah, but—" She stared up through the branches and the haze, trying to locate the winged creatures. "You didn't say there were flying monkeys here."

"Monkeys?" He followed her gaze upwards. "Those aren't monkeys. They're sentries."

She squinted into the sky and saw the creatures in a tight-knit formation, making a beeline toward the raging sunset. Eunice scrabbled over a block of asphalt and joined Joseph.

"What does my mother need sentries for?"

"They're not your mother's."

Eunice peered at Joseph.

He replied, "Someone else is worried about you, Eunice. They don't want you here."

For a moment, she stood stunned. *Someone else is worried about you.* What was that supposed to mean? Who could be that worried about her? And what were they doing in her mother's world? The raging sun. The tree of death. The winged sentries. And now, an angry watcher bent on sending her packing. She wasn't a genius, but it didn't take one to know that this trip would only get worse.

As Eunice struggled to suppress a rising dread, something moved ahead of them—something squat and nervous and completely inhuman. Her breath caught in her throat. For underneath the rancid tree scurried a creature that looked, for the life of her, like the largest grub the world had ever seen.

FIVE

Joseph seemed unafraid of the creature under the black tree. He leapt over a growth of roots and then turned back to Eunice and motioned her forward. Yet she dared not move.

"Don't be scared," he urged. "He won't bite."

Eunice gulped. "You sure about that?"

"Positive. He might slobber on you and he smells pretty bad. But he won't bite."

She scowled at Joseph.

Upon closer inspection, the creature was neither human nor insect, but a deranged hybrid of species. An immense droopy head with thick jowls lolled atop a soft arachnid-like torso. It wore filthy jean overalls and waddled upright on two stumpy legs. Four gangly arms, each with a claw-like hand, pattered nervously about the creature's body—scratching, touching, and kneading its gelatinous torso. The grub man shambled about in the most awkward fashion, plopping onto the ground in a snuffling heap, before scurrying to its feet again to begin its worried march.

Suddenly, the creature looked at them. Sallow eyes lay sunken under dense overgrown brows—a face that could have been that of an old man. It glanced their way and began sloughing and scuttling more the earnest, flashing a worrisome gaze.

Eunice clambered over several roots and joined Joseph, and together they stood watching the grub-man. Finally, she leaned over and whispered, "What's he doing?"

"What he was born to do."

The creature kept groveling and glancing their way. Suddenly, he plopped onto the ground, crossed his four arms, and yowled, "I ain't goin'! D'ya hear? I ain't goin'!"

Eunice whispered to Joseph. "Where isn't he going?"

"With us."

"With us?!" she blurted. "Why would he—? I don't want that thing comin' with us."

"You don't have a choice. Your mother's tying up loose ends. And he's one of them. He *has* to come. And you're his escort. In fact, here he comes now."

Instantly, the creature was upon them.

He stomped his feet and his face grew long and pouty. "Why? Why do they always do it? Mmph! These last minute reprieves are wrong, Joe—dead wrong."

"It's her call, Mordant," Joseph said flatly.

"I knew it," the creature bawled. Then he crossed his arms and tamped the ground like a sulking child. "Oh-h, I knew she'd do it. Fried and frazzled. Pffh! It's the way of nature, it is. Nothing lasts. Nothing! And the lovelies—they all turns to rot. And the sun—even that's gonna go! Gaw-w-w! Doomed—we're all doomed."

Joseph shook his head at the creature's melodramatic presentation. "I'm sorry, but you had your chance. Now it's time to go."

"Chance?" the grub man sniveled. "What chance? Never really had a chance. Things'r set. Drawn'n quartered. Predestined, we are. No room for chance. Rftt! The rot—it kills you, kills you good. Ain't my fault. No. *Stir the pot and serve the stew*, that's my motto. Can't blame Mordant for the taste. Not Mordant! It's the rot. Blame the lovelies. The lovelies got the rot."

Eunice may have drooled upon herself, so great was her stupefaction with the grub man. However, when she glanced at Joseph, he just stood tapping his foot impatiently.

"It's not a fair playing field any more, Joe." The creature pointed an accusatory finger at Joseph. "But how would you know? Huh? Up there all special. Mmph! Gotta birds-eye view. Ain't down here ing the ruination. And them—" he jabbed his thumb toward Eunice. "The lovelies get the breaks. Chance. Pah! The only ones with a chance are you."

Then he muttered something and began nervously kneading his abdomen. "Knew it. I just knew it."

"Get your stuff," said Joseph to the worrisome creature. "C'mon, sun's setting. We ain't got forever."

But the creature just grumbled and started tromping back-and-forth again, his face drawn in near-comedic misery.

Eunice looked quizzically at Joseph. He sighed heavily and then nodded to her, and she seemed to know what he was thinking. So she cleared her throat and wobbled forward. "Listen, y-you," she said to the pitiful creature. "She w-wants you, so...you're comin' with me."

Eunice glanced again at Joseph. This time he arched his eyebrows and a surprised grin creased his lips.

But the grub ignored Eunice and continued grousing about misfortune, fallen empires, and the deck being stacked against him. "Knew it. I knew she'd do it. Grff!. Doomed I was, from the beginning."

Eunice looked once more at Joseph for assistance, but he had stepped in a pile of rotten fruit and was busy knocking gooey clods from his heel. So she cleared her throat again and tried to muster a little more authority. "Look, you! You're coming with—"

"Who're you?" snapped the grub man, glaring rather menacingly from under immense calloused brows.

Eunice stumbled backward, startled by the creature's response.

"Don't start that, Mordant." Joseph looked up from scraping his shoe on a chunk of concrete. "You know who she is."

Eunice glanced between the two of them, but the creature had his hands on his hips and was glowering, waiting for her reply.

Eunice shrugged. "Me? I-I'm—" she sputtered. "No! Who're you?"

"Like you don't know."

"W-well, I... I don't."

"Oh, I get it," whined the grub man. "I'm the stranger again."

Then he stopped and his tone grew grave. "Can't shake it that easy, Missy. When it's nature, you can't shake it at all."

Missy? Eunice caught herself gaping at this fount of pessimism and worry. He seemed so familiar; his words stirred an intangible pang, an ache that she couldn't quite finger. And that name...

"I d-don't...," she stammered. "What're you saying?"

Suddenly he scuttled closer, close enough that she could smell the stink of bog and fetid earth on his flesh. A lattice of fine veins was visible under his skin, and his jowls trembled. She instinctively clasped her hand over her nose, partly for fear that he would reach out and touch her with one of those buggy paws. Instead, he tapped his forehead and whispered, "In there, locked up. The stew—it's waiting to be stirred."

Then he tromped back and resumed his gloomy lamentation. "There's laws for it. Calibrations of some sort. Thistle, thastle, brastle, pfffh!" His arms gestured wildly in several directions and saliva sprayed the air. "Things break. Crash and crumble. Brph! And then the weeds. Oh-h, the weeds come up and the bad seed blooms. Just look." He spread his arms and gestured to the cancerous tree and the fuming horizon. "The poison... Awwkh! The *poison*. But you know—mmph!—can't pretend. The rot—it's done you in." He doubled over with his hand on his stomach. "Oh-h-h! Done us all in."

Eunice stared, both mystified and repulsed by this melancholy troll. Finally, she said, "I'm not sure I like you"

"I don't blame you," he moaned. "Don't blame you at all. What's to like? But you—you got the medicine, don't ya, Missy? Roots and gills and pretty pills. Numbs the pain. The pain... O-o-oh! We knows the pain. Don't we, Missy?"

The medicine? How did he—? She glared at him. "Now I'm positive I don't like you. Who are you?"

"Mordant," he snapped. "Mister Mordant. I was the emperor here. Once. I was the king."

"Mordant?" Eunice scowled at the creature. "Why, I-I've never—I have no idea who you are."

"Get your stuff," said Joseph to Mister Mordant, shaking the final clods of fruit from his shoes. "You know the drill. Whatever she left you with—.

"Nothin'! She left me nothin' 'cept this ulcer. Gaw-w-w..." He pressed his palms to his stomach and made an awful face. "Shoulda known. Thorns and thistles. Pfft! Doomed. I was doomed from the start."

"Alright then," said Joseph. "Say goodbye to—" he stared up into the tree and grimaced, "to home."

Then something happened that totally caught Eunice off guard. Mordant's eyes pooled with tears and he began sniffling and pressing in upon her, wringing his hands in anguish. "It's a mistake, Missy. Tell her it's a m-mistake." His chest heaved and a terrible trembling overtook him. He wiped his snotty nose and slurped, "Can't j-just lemme go. We was friends. All of us. Oh-h-rt! It's a m-mistake. Tell 'er."

Then he turned and scuttled back into a burrow at the base of the tree. Ducking inside, he snuffled about, and then peered at them with sad, languid eyes.

But at the moment, Eunice did not feel sympathy for Mister Mordant. In fact, something he said had sent gooseflesh skittering across her forearms. For now, she remembered that name.

"What'd you call me?" Eunice cautiously approached the earthen hovel. "That name…"

Mordant dabbed his eyes and sniffled. Then he slunk deeper into the hole, looking rather frightened.

"You called me *Missy*. My mother was the only one who ever called me that. And I didn't like it." Eunice leaned forward, squinting at Mordant. "*Who are you?*"

"You'll have plenty of time to get reacquainted," Joseph said. "Now come on." And he turned and began walking into the gloomy basin.

Eunice stood there at the base of the monstrous black tree, studying this strange being huddled, sniveling, in its burrow. *Missy.* The mention of that name sent her mind reeling. Memories from her past—memories of the most awful kind—seemed to reawaken with a newfound life. What else did this thing know about her?

Mordant peeked tentatively from inside the lair. "But we was friends," he mewed.

"Yeah? Well, not any more." Then she pointed in Joseph's direction. "After you... *Mister Mordant.*"

Mordant grumbled something, burst out of the burrow, and scurried after Joseph on his stubby legs.

Eunice watched the two of them make their way through the wretched minefield of roots and splattered pods, back onto the highway—Joseph limping in methodical rhythm, and Mordant commiserating with himself in animated discussion.

The fiery-ringed sun looked larger now, consuming most of the horizon. What awaited her there? What other surprises might she encounter in this strange inner world? And how much more *personal* was this going to get?

Missy. Eunice hadn't heard that name in 20 years. But the monsters that name summoned provoked a fear that no diseased tree or grotesque grub could eclipse.

She stood alone under the black tree and looked up into the gnarled branches. Its shade cast an oppressive pall over this place, and disease oozed from the earth like radioactive waste from a nuclear meltdown.

Eunice prepared to hurry off, when a breeze drifted across the asphalt, stirring the haze and rattling the branches. The grim distant moaning rose and, for the first time, she recognized it as voices—a legion of sobs and wails joined in some dread chorus. Eunice peered back up at the brooding tree.

Fight. Yes, she could do that.

Eunice shivered and bustled over the roots and cracked asphalt toward her companions, anxious to leave the shadow of the devil tree. However, she couldn't help but wonder if its disease had already poisoned her.

SIX

"Follow the stream," Joseph called over his shoulder, maintaining his methodical, determined, pace.

The stream, however, was nothing more than a black rivulet that twined its way through the asphalt, a vein of toxic sludge oozing downward into the smog-shrouded basin. Knowing the source of this rancid liquid made the process all the more difficult for Eunice. The smell of the rotten fruit—the spring from which this black brook originated—seemed to wrap her in a funk. Eunice found herself fending off ghosts from her past she'd believed were long since exorcised.

Mordant kept glancing back over his shoulder at Eunice, twitching, slurping, and making all manner of ghastly noises. Who was this creature? And what did he know about her and her past? She had a mind to query him, drill him for answers. Yet engaging a worrisome, arachnid-like old man who knew too much about her, was about as thrilling as swan-diving into a sewer.

The highway continued its descent into the hazy basin. Along the way, they passed random debris: a twisted fender, a rusted speed limit sign, shards of broken mirror and stray lug nuts. As disconcerting as it was to come upon evidences of wreckage in this dreamworld, it seemed to quell some of her unease. Whatever this place was, it was somehow connected to hers, as if the two worlds had overlapped and she was traversing a seam. Maybe that's why Joseph had described it as a crossroad or intersection. Yet the possibility that her world—the real world—was interlaced with this one did not eliminate her fears. It did, however, keep her from wanting to click her heels three times and return to the pileup on the 210. At least, for the moment.

Joseph remained a short distance ahead of them, but his pace had intensified. From here, his limp appeared even worse.

Yet he had no problem outdistancing Eunice and the muttering Mordant.

Despite Joseph's exhortations to not over-think things, Eunice found herself in an anxious loop, wondering at the images Mister Mordant seemed to have conjured within her. Finally, she made up her mind to explore the issue with her guide. Drawing a deep breath, she jogged past the creature who issued a surprised grunt as she passed.

"We need to talk." She came alongside Joseph, panting.

"You did good back there," he said.

"Huh?"

"You know, telling him he's coming with us. That was good. Taking charge like that could be helpful around here."

"Uh, I'll keep that in mind."

Joseph continued trudging forward and Eunice scrambled to keep up with him.

Finally, she said, "Listen, can you slow down just a bit?"

He glanced at her without responding or interrupting his pace in the least. If a power-walking contest was ever held in Winterland, she was sure he would be a finalist.

"Hello?" she said. "Earth to Joseph. Can you slow down?"

"No," he said flatly. "That's what he wants."

"Who?"

"Mordant." Joseph's tone was stern. "He wants you to slow down. In fact, he wants you to stop—can't you see that? Things like him don't survive by moving."

She glanced over her shoulder at the mumbling grub man and cringed at the thought. "Okay, I guess we'll keep moving."

"That's what I thought. Sometimes it's the only thing you can do to survive. You know—one foot in front of the other. Keep breathing. Keep moving. Because if you listen to him long enough, you'll wanna stop. Trust me. You'll wanna pull up a chair and have a pity party and just stop trying all together. In fact, jumping off an overpass might seem like a reasonable option. Not many people can listen to him and move on. It's a miracle your mother ever did."

She had never viewed her mother's life in terms of something miraculous.

Eunice glanced back at Mordant. "He can do that? Then why're we bringing him with us? Can't we just, like, think him into the cornfield or something?"

"Funny." Joseph shook his head. "Naw. Some bonds can't be broken that easy. Besides, this isn't your world, Eunice. You've been granted access. Blessed, you could say. But your mother has nurtured Mordant far too long. And the longer you let it live, the stronger it gets. And the more personal."

The last thing she needed right now was for things to get more personal. She shook her head, struggling both to comprehend Joseph's enigmatic answers and to keep up with him. Behind them, Mister Mordant grumbled something about being overmatched and outnumbered, and the inevitability of his demise. Did she really want to go on with this?

Without looking at her, Joseph said, "And you should stop biting your nails."

A flush of embarrassment swept over her. Eunice wiped her fingers on her jeans and forced her arm to her side. The habit had returned with a vengeance.

"Listen," said Eunice. "You said you'd help me."

"I *am* helping you."

"Yeah, but..." Eunice wheezed. "You talk in riddles. Can't you just give me a straight answer?"

"My answers only seem like riddles to you because you've spent so much of your life avoiding the answers."

"Avoiding the answers?" She scowled and said defensively, "Rehab wasn't exactly avoiding answers. Sheesh!"

Joseph looked sideways at her and then conceded, "You're right. It was a good start."

"Gee, thanks."

Despite turning pouty, Eunice knew Joseph was right. Rehab was a great start. Nevertheless, she had spent her life avoiding the answers, hiding behind chemicals and regrets. Grousing about the childhood that should have been. Fessing up to her addictions was just the beginning of the process.

"Listen," Joseph said, as if he sensed her drifting off into a funk. "Right now, your mother's inspired from your efforts. She's proud of you. You can take heart in that. The only problem is she's made a mess of things. There's so much junk to maneuver just to get to her. Either way, if you just stay on it and if you can get to the end of this highway, my riddles will make perfectly good sense. All right?"

She stared into the growing grey looming ahead of them. The notion that her mother was actually inspired by Eunice's stay in drug rehab struck her as rather astounding. At death's door, things like this probably happened. Remorse. Contrition. Then again, maybe her mother was just medicated out of her mind.

"Okay. I'll try," she said, glancing back at Mordant. "But I wish he didn't have to come with us. He gives me the creeps." She forced an exaggerated shiver. "And how does he know so much about me?"

"This is the way she came, Eunice. What she knows, he knows. They're related in ways you can't imagine."

"Related?! That's an awful thought."

"You ain't kidding. But if you're gonna save her, you have to bring him. That's what she wants. She's gotta be the one to sign off on his claim. But I have to warn you—he knows a lot more about the two of you than you realize."

"That's comforting." Eunice cringed at the thought. "My mother—she's the one who used to call me Missy. Actually, it was *Miss E*—as in the letter E. That's what it stood for. It just came out as *Missy* to everyone else. But she was the only one who called me that. Her," Eunice glanced at Joseph, "and the men she... *serviced.*"

Joseph looked sideways at her.

"She had to pay the bills, and after my dad left..." Eunice shrugged.

A moment of uncomfortable silence passed between them. How long had it been since Eunice mentioned—even hinted at—her mother's prostitution? She quickly turned and stared blankly down the road.

"Ooch!" Mordant suddenly shrieked. "Prickly dingles! Help! Help me!"

At the sound of his awful, helium-high shriek, Eunice spun around to see the creature tamping the ground with his feet, his arms flailing in panic.

"What is it?" Eunice cried. "What's wrong?"

Mordant frantically jabbed his hands towards the foggy road ahead of them and sputtered, "Musn't go! Musn't go! Mmph! Worse than Mordant!"

"What's he talking about?"

"Monsters!" Mordant bawled. "Barbs and choppers. Br-r-rph! Downstream—no place for pretties. No!"

She turned to Joseph for help, when Mordant lunged toward Eunice pleadingly. "Please, Missy! We can..." He began scanning the area. "We can stay. Here, look!" He began gathering debris, scuttling about like some lunatic ant, assembling a crude pile. "A fire—see? Settle in. Warm the bones. Br-r-r." He shook his jowls, then issued a sad smile and gazed longingly at Eunice.

Eunice peered at Mordant, and then turned to Joseph. "What's he afraid of?"

"The Trench," Joseph said somberly. "He knows it's coming."

Eunice gazed back down the road. "The Trench?"

"It happened when she was young," Joseph said. "Nothing but a swamp now. A really awful swamp, at that."

She turned back to Mordant who had plopped onto the ground with his legs crossed Indian style, and sat rubbing his hands together as if he were warming himself at an invisible fire.

"What're you doing?" she said.

Mordant looked up at her with puppy dog eyes.

"No," said Eunice emphatically. "We are not staying."

"Oh-h-h. Please!" Mordant scrambled to his feet and approached her with a pitiful groveling. "Trouble ahead. Fights and fizzles. Mmph! Big trouble!"

Joseph stood watching them intently, as if her next move were of utmost importance.

"We're not staying." Eunice straightened and looked down the highway. "My mother wants you, so you're coming with me."

Suddenly a drift of fog wafted by and Mordant wailed at its chilly touch.

"Eunice!"

It was Joseph. She turned to the space where he'd been, but he was gone.

"Eunice!"

She squinted up ahead, but the landscape seemed to have changed. Either that or someone was tinkering with her point of view. Eunice took a deep breath and closed her eyes. When she reopened them, Joseph now stood on what appeared to be a precipice, his hair gusting about his face. He motioned her forward.

Somehow, she knew Mordant must follow her. So Eunice began trudging toward Joseph. Making her way past huge slabs of upturned asphalt, she reached the rim of a great chasm and stood next to her guide, gaping. An immense fault line appeared to have cleaved the highway. Perhaps two hundred feet below them the highway descended into a basin of mist. It was the Trench. Twisted tree limbs rose from this languid sea of fog and behind it, the ringed sun stared on like an unblinking eye. The distant melancholy moan began, echoing across the vast gray horizon.

"It's the swamp of Mlaise," Joseph said somberly.

She looked at him, incredulous.

He raised his hand, as if to stop her. "Don't even say it."

"We're supposed to hike through *that?* And do it by nightfall?" Eunice shook her head in dismay. "And I get how many chances?"

"This is it." Joseph started angling his way down the crumbling escarpment.

Eunice watched and then called after him, "Can I at least get some better shoes?"

"You have everything you need," Joseph responded. "Just keep moving forward. That's all you ever need to do."

SEVEN

They scrabbled downward through boulders and black earth. Eunice's eyes burned. The swamp reeked of chemical toxins and vegetative mold. Mordant's warning about monsters had set her on edge and she kept stopping to gaze down into the gloom of Mlaise. If this really was her mother's world, she could only imagine the types of beasts that lived here. Mister Mordant was proof of that.

They reached the bottom and Eunice hunched forward, panting, with her hands on knees. Mordant collapsed nearby and sat whining about ulcers, blisters, and the unfairness of destiny.

"If this is a dream," Eunice wheezed, "it's an awfully tiring one."

But Joseph did not reply. He stood fixated forward. Eunice straightened and followed his gaze to see a bank of fog, a solid curtain of roiling mist, swallowing the highway, barreling toward them like a spectral tide.

"This looks bad." Joseph seized her forearm. "Whatever you do, do not leave the stream. Do you hear me?"

"But I—"

"Do you hear me?" Joseph demanded.

She turned and watched as the cloudy veil bore down on them. "Yes. I hear you."

"If we get separated, keep following the stream. No matter what he says."

"Me?" Mordant squalled. "Why me?"

"Stay to the stream," Joseph said, ignoring the grub man. "Do you understand?"

The thought of being alone in the fog, in this god-awful netherworld with Mister Mordant made her cringe. "Yes," she said. "I hear you. But I don't plan on getting separated. Do you?"

He didn't answer.

"And I can still go back, right?"

Yet Joseph had tilted forward, bracing himself against the onrushing wall of fog.

Mlaise swept over them like a ghostly current, biting through her clothing and stinging her flesh. With it came a blinding gray. Mordant shrieked from somewhere nearby. Eunice peered into the mist, wincing at its spray, holding her breath as the gloom enveloped them. Winterland disappeared. The charred asphalt. The black stream. The burning sky. All was swallowed in the noxious haze. Except for the patter of moisture, her mother's world went strangely silent.

"Joseph?" Eunice finally whispered.

But there was only the murmur of mist.

"Joseph." She groped blindly into the murk, growing more frantic. "Joseph!"

"I'm right here." He put his hand on her shoulder.

She jolted and then slumped forward in relief.

Together they turned and stared into the swamp of Mlaise. As her eyes adjusted, shadowy forms began to take shape around them, outlines of withered trees tilted between slabs of upturned road. A soft chirring, as that of insects, droned to life. The stillness seemed to awaken the world.

"This is the way she came." Joseph's tone was dour.

"How did she ever make it through this?"

"Beats me. But you should be thankful she did."

Thankful? That notion had never crossed Eunice's mind and confronting it here, in the face of this dismal marsh, seemed all the more revelatory.

Mordant's bleating had descended into an incessant whimper. She could hear him squirming around on the moist tarmac nearby. His agitation grated on her nerves. Trudging through this swamp was bad enough without having to listen to his tortured sniveling.

As if sensing her annoyance, Joseph said, "We gotta keep moving. It's worse when you stand still."

"Burrows," Mordant moaned. "Brph! Needs the burrows."

She heard him scramble to his feet.

"We're not finding any burrows," Eunice growled. "Now, c'mon."

"The stream is that way." Joseph pointed. "We can—"

"Mordant finds 'em! Yes! Leads the way." The grub man waddled out of the fog, wringing his hands. "I was emperor once, 'member? Know the nooks and grottos."

"No," Eunice snapped. "If my mother made it, then we can make it. Now stop your—"

"Doomed!" Mordant bawled. "We're all doomed! Dust and bones, that's our lot. Phft! The pretty's lost her sense. Temptin' fate, she is. Oh-h-h. Fate—it's a twisty one. And nature. Can't win there. Fate 'n nature. Fate 'n nature. No sir."

Eunice stood gritting her teeth at Mordant's bellyaching.

"Fate 'n nature," Mordant carped. "Ain't no winnin'! We're at their mercy. All of us! Waste and wither. Grrrph! No fightin' the tide. Futile, it is. *The tide*—you felt it, Missy. Tides'o comin'. Ain't my fault. I just stir the pot and serve the stew. That's my motto. Blame the pretties. They let the—"

"Would you shut up!" Eunice snapped. "Geez! It's bad enough we can't see anything. Listening to you only make things worse."

Mordant stumbled backwards, his eyes swollen in shock.

Eunice glared at him. "So what? So what if fate and nature's against us, huh? We're supposed to just roll over? Life sucks and then you die?" Eunice swiped her hand through the air in disgust. "No wonder my mother went nuts. Listening to you, who wouldn't?"

The creature's mouth quivered.

Her heart drummed in her temples. A flush of embarrassment swept over Eunice. She was startled by her outburst. Her mother had always been a sucker for sorrow and self-pity, the perpetual family martyr. Eunice couldn't stand it then, and she couldn't stand it now. Nevertheless, she mustn't allow this creature to get under her skin.

The grub man slowly retreated into the fog, muttering to himself.

"C'mon," Joseph finally said. "Let's get going."

She peered at the shadowy silhouette of the miserable creature. Then she sighed heavily, and nodded. "Right."

As they went, the visibility increased enough to make out the swampy terrain. Skeletal stalks rising between asphalt fissures revealed a perpetual autumn. Her hair began to tangle and drip moisture. Their words and movements, even the sticky coiling of the stream, was amplified in that gloomy tent.

She thought about her Audi station wagon on the 210 freeway and the traffic jam she had left. Joseph had assured her it was not far away. Maybe it was still right here, in some strange parallel dimension. But even that assurance could not dissuade her of some immanent madness.

Joseph finally located the stream, yet it was barely a yard's width and little more than black sludge. The stench returned and she curdled her nose at the reminder of the pestilent tree that fed this rivulet. Dark roots snaked their way upward, forming columns and tiers along the shoreline before rising into the fog. Sheer pale flowers budded against the black wood, swaying like ghostly anemones in an invisible ocean.

They walked on, following the slurry brook as it descended into Mlaise.

The surreal landscape seeped into her psyche. It seemed as though time stood still here, as if the fog had not just shrouded them, but cocooned her in a distant dream.

Missy.

She had done her best to force that name from her mind. Yet Mordant had pried it free like a fossil from some ancient strata. Though she tried to resist the temptation, Eunice found herself listening to the creature as he dawdled behind them.

Who was he? How was he attached to her family? And had he really altered the course of their lives? His groans and grousing were an ever-present reminder of his proximity, and a reminder of the terminal pessimism which had poisoned her mother.

She watched Joseph plod through the gloom ahead, disquiet coiling about her…

…and then a tune, faint and airy, caught her attention.

"I was standing by the window
On a cold and cloudy day
When I saw the hearse come rolling
To carry my mother away."

It was distant, but unmistakable. The old hymn from her childhood. And the voice was that of a child.

"Who is that?" She stopped, turned, and peered into the gray curtain, mesmerized by the distant minstrel. "Who is that singing?"

"Oomph!" Mordant stumbled to a stop behind her, muttering to himself.

She craned forward. "That voice. It sounds familiar."

"Will the circle be unbroken
Bye and bye Lord bye and bye
There's a better home a waiting
In the sky, Lord, in the sky."

"It's Emma," Mordant said, surprise in his tone. "She made it. Hmmph!"

"Emma?" she said, dreamily.

The name seemed to awaken some long-forgotten ethos, like a curio unearthed from a dusty bin, or a picture from one's childhood.

Emma. Of course.

Eunice's family had an unusual affinity for *E* names. Aunt Ellie. Uncle Ern. Eunice's sister, Emerald. And of course, her mother. Eunice thought it was weird and often vowed that, if she ever had children, she would stay as far away from E names as possible. At the moment, *William* and *Zoë* were high on her list.

"Emma?" Eunice peered at Mister Mordant. "You don't mean…?"

He stood terribly poised, peering at some distant point in the fog.

"Granny Em. That's what I used to call her." She followed his gaze into the gloom. Then she said absently, "She killed herself, you know."

EIGHT

Two things happened simultaneously, neither of which struck Eunice as peculiar. The moment she realized they had wandered from the stream and that Joseph was nowhere to be found, the fog parted to reveal a quaint cottage with warm lights glowing through steamy panes. Perhaps she had mistakenly wandered into Thomas Kinkade's world along the way.

Eunice stared at the cottage. It looked familiar. The singing came from here, and now she knew it was not that of a child.

> *"I said to the undertaker*
> *Undertaker please drive slow*
> *For this lady you are carrying*
> *Lord I hate to see her go."*

"That voice." Eunice cocked her head. "I know that voice."

"'Course you do," Mordant said distantly.

For some reason it did not seem odd to Eunice, this house in the fog on a highway of dreams. The melancholy tune and the glowing warmth. It was as if some long-forgotten chord was being strummed deep inside her.

Maybe this journey was not about her mother at all.

She meandered forward, studying the house. Flowering vines in lush shades of blue and violet graced its footings, grappling up tilted trellises and twining into the dank air. She did not bother to ask how such a dreary world could sustain such rich foliage, for the house seemed like such an oddity, something straight out of a nursery rhyme or gothic poem. And the singing…

> *"Will the circle be unbroken*
> *Bye and bye Lord, bye and bye*
> *There's a better home a waiting*
> *In the sky Lord in the sky"*

Moisture etched the panes, the droplets sparkling like honey from the interior glow. Eunice moved closer, drawn by the song. As she approached, she detected movement inside. Eunice approached the window, cupping her hands about her face in order to see inside. Someone sat before a crackling fire, rocking methodically.

"Who could that be," Eunice said. "Out here all alone?"

She swiped condensation from the window, and peered at the silhouette. But she could not make out the singer.

A bank of fog swept by, rocking the tendrils overhead. Drizzle came with it. Eunice shivered. Perhaps she could warm herself inside just long enough to regain strength for this dreadful journey of hers.

"Granny Em," Mordant whispered from behind Eunice. "Mother never wanted 'er to leave."

"That's not a surprise." Eunice stepped away from the window. "Granny Em never seemed at home over there." She began meandering around the cottage. "It's not the kinda family history someone wants to talk about, ya know? I stayed with her when I was a kid. She was a neat old lady. Eccentric, but kind. She always liked that creepy old hymn about death and dying. About unbroken circles and stuff. I didn't think anything of it, till she—" Eunice stopped, perhaps fifteen feet from the door of the house. "Granny Em started to cut herself. Self-mutilation, they called it. Mother finally put her in an institution. I never visited her there. Couldn't bring myself to do it. Felt pretty guilty about it, too."

Mordant was behind her now, unusually quiet.

"They found her dead one day," Eunice said. "Curled up in her own vomit. Drank drain cleaner, or something."

The asphalt was no longer visible, and the ground was speckled with moss and brackish puddles. Stepping-stones traced a path into the house. Eunice remembered playing hopscotch, as a child, along these same stones. The back door was open and Eunice crept toward it. As she did, the singer's voice resumed.

"Well I followed close behind her
Tried to hold up and be brave
But I could not hide my sorrow
When they laid her in that grave."

Eunice did not need to look behind her, for she could feel Mordant following closely. His groveling had changed and become a dissonant guttural hum. However, despite her repulsion of the grub man, the mystery of it all carried her forward.

Besides, she could return whenever she wanted.

Eunice stepped into the doorway.

The cottage was exactly as she remembered it, cluttered and warm. Dusty antiques and quilts in mid progress scattered the place. Her wooden rocker was near the fireplace, Granny Em's favorite spot. Someone sat there, back turned to Eunice, with a sheet of fabric draped over their legs. As Eunice entered the doorway, the figure stopped rocking and straightened.

"Granny Em?" Eunice's breath caught in her throat. "Is that you?"

She needn't have asked that question. The long-sleeved lacy dress, white hair drawn back into a tight ponytail, yellowed from age—there was no mistaking it. This was her grandmother.

But why was Granny Em living inside Eunice's mother's world?

Eunice could smell Mordant's moldy breath over her shoulder. He was mumbling something about stews and stirring and rot recurring. As she stepped into the cottage, the woman set aside the quilt and stood. But she did not face Eunice.

She simply stood with her back turned.

"Granny Em?" Eunice inched forward. "Why're you here?"

But the woman remained looking the opposite direction.

"Granny Em?" Eunice angled her way past a roll-top desk. "It's me, Eunice. That you?"

Yet the old woman continued to face the opposite direction. Then the song started again:

"Will the circle be unbroken
Bye and bye Lord, bye and bye
There's a better home a waiting
In the sky Lord, in the sky"

But the singing did not come from the woman. An old record player, its stylus bobbing atop a warped vinyl album, sat in the corner. It was a gospel choir, she guessed. When Eunice came to this realization, the woman turned to face her.

Eunice stopped in her tracks.

For she still saw the woman's back.

"Granny Em?" Eunice squinted, trying to compute what had just happened. "Look at me."

Granny Em turned again, and Eunice's stomach dropped. There was no mistaking it. The woman's front... *was another back.*

Eunice stumbled backwards, colliding with Mordant who snuffled excitedly. Perhaps it was an optical illusion, as so much of Winterland appeared to be. Yet Eunice was sure the woman had turned around. Twice. Nevertheless, the woman's elbows, palms, heels, and white ponytail still faced Eunice. She'd heard of people being two-faced, but *no-faced* was another category.

Her grandmother was the Lady of the Perpetual Back.

A wave of nausea tightened Eunice's stomach. For the inverted person was walking toward Eunice. The movement was wholly unnerving, giving the appearance that Granny Em—or whatever Granny Em had become—was walking backwards.

Eunice shook her head. "The circle," she muttered, edging toward the doorway. "The unbroken circle. It needs to be broken. The circle *needs* to be broken."

Mordant yelped as Eunice fled from the warm cottage into the fog.

"Joseph!" she skidded to a stop, peering into the mist. "Joseph! God, what've I done?"

Mordant waddled after her, blathering about the benefits of immobility.

"The stream," she said frantically, scanning the clearing. "The stream!"

A flutter of wings sounded. Wooden branches snapped and tumbled to the ground. She stumbled back as the harpies burst from the treetops and disappeared into the fog.

"Joseph!" Eunice called. "Help!"

She ran blindly, Granny Em's empty face burning holes into her brain. What did it mean? Was it really her? The hellish opera began its symphony, filling the air with distant shrieks. She dodged leafless trees and hurdled chunks of asphalt in the direction she believed she'd last come.

"I can go back," she panted. "I can go back."

As she was about to cry out for help again, Eunice smashed into something and fell flat on her back.

She groaned and raised herself on her elbows. Her forehead throbbed. Yet the fog cleared enough to make out a vast tower rising precariously into the flaming sky. She'd run square into a lighthouse. An obelisk. And from a window, high above, someone was watching her.

NINE

Eunice lay on her back, massaging her forehead and checking her fingertips for blood. But there was no time to worry over her physical state. She blinked hard, then traced the white crumbling wall with her eyes, higher and higher. The tower tilted precariously, shifting in the breeze, creaking and groaning something terrible. Chunks of plaster and stone clattered to the base of the structure.

"How'd you—?" Joseph stood panting before her, appearing as if out of nowhere. "You found it!"

"Did I?" she said woozily.

The fog was gone, as was the Swamp of Mlaise. Eunice bolted to her feet, scanning her surroundings. Before her, an arid plain now stretched. A stone archway teetered there and behind it, the tarry rivulet cut a path into the parched ground, a black vein tracing its way down the gray earth to the basin. Behind her, the misty shroud of Mlaise had withdrawn and draped the withered treeline like a curtain. How had she gotten here? And where was she?

"I thought I'd lost you," Joseph said.

"You did," Eunice answered sarcastically.

"I told you not to listen to him. So how'd you find your way?"

"I dunno. I guess a cottage on the freeway in the fog with my dead grandmother isn't exactly my picture of a dream house." Then she stared up at the tower. "But what exactly have I found?"

"It's the Plains of Cinder," Joseph motioned to the broad flat basin that now stretched before them. "And this," he pointed to the rickety spire, "is the Tower of Industry. Built exclusively by one Reverend Ash."

Eunice peered at Joseph. "Ash?"

"*Reverend* Ash," Joseph said with exaggerated haughtiness. "He's particular about that."

"I suppose that was him up there." She pointed toward the window in the tower. It was empty.

Without looking, Joseph nodded. "He knew we were coming. He's been watching us. And he won't like the idea of having to come down."

Eunice put her hands on her hips and glared at Joseph.

He shrugged. "Your mother wants him. What can I say? He's not gonna come down on his own. They never do." Joseph moved a step closer, a sparkle in his bad eye. "It's why you're here, Eunice. You're supposed to do this." Then he stepped back, brushing nonchalantly at his clothing. "Besides, like I said, you can leave whenever you want."

"I'm not sure I like that option anymore."

"Why? Because there's no risk involved?"

"No. Because it's too tempting."

Joseph arched his eyebrows. "Would you rather have no freedom?"

She looked at him long and hard. "Anyway. So who is he?"

"No!" Mordant sloughed up from behind her, casting a frightful gaze up at the looming tower. "Missy! You don't understand. It's Ash's fault. All of this! Woulda never happened without him. Prpff! He started the whole thing!"

She extended her hand to halt his advance.

"Brrph!" Mordant stumbled to stop. "He stole 'er! Didn't play fair. Mlaise—it woulda never happened. Uh-uh! Ash's fault, I tell ya. See? Ya got the wrong one, Missy. The wrong one. Mordant can go free. Back to burrow. Ash—he's the one you want!" He pointed all four of his hands up at the tower and spat.

Eunice peered at him. "I told you to stop calling me Missy."

A proud smile blossomed on Joseph's face.

Mordant huffed and turned away pouting.

Eunice heaved a great sigh and looked at Joseph. "Is she up there?"

"Your mother? Oh, no. She's at the end of the road. It's just him—Reverend Ash. He doesn't share Industry with anyone. It's all him."

She cast a dark silent look at the precarious structure. "So what do I have to do?"

"You have to go up and get him."

"Go up *there*?"

He nodded.

"That's what I thought." She drew a deep breath. "Okay. You're coming, right?"

"Of course!" Joseph clicked his heels.

"And him?" Eunice motioned to Mister Mordant. The creature stumbled forward, wringing his hands, pleading with Eunice to have mercy on him. She silenced him and without waiting for Joseph's response, said, "All right, he's coming."

"Ain't made for heights. Ert! Mordant can't climb!"

"Well," Eunice said, "Mordant's gonna learn."

Joseph led the way around the structure and as he did, a great gust of arid air blew up from the plains and struck them. The awful sun flared on the horizon and the Tower of Industry shifted, its timber and plaster dissenting against the blast. Eunice shielded her eyes against twigs and particles of sand. As the gale died, she looked behind her. Mlaise had vanished. Was it ever really there to begin with? Together, their gazes rose up, up into the fiery sky of Winterland, to the tilted spire.

"This thing's gonna collapse," Eunice said.

"You would think."

"And someone lives here?"

"It's amazing what people learn to tolerate, isn't it?"

Eunice scowled at Joseph.

He began hiking around the perimeter of Industry, picking through the debris until they reached a massive wooden door, tall and narrow.

"What's that?" Eunice leaned closer.

On the door hung a long scroll, consisting of what appeared to be lists. At the top of each page, in large handwritten letters, were the words

RULES FOR ENTRY

After which followed an itemization of requirements. She cleared her throat and read aloud, "Hygienics: Wash hands. Trim nails. Deposit nails appropriately. Wash hands again, giving attention to cuticle depth. Trim nails again, as needed. Antisepticise. Proceed to fumigation. Huh?" She looked at her hands. They were filthy from the bog and several nails were broken. But it would take more than a pedicure to comply with these demands. She continued reading, her tone growing more perturbed. "Inspect clothing. If any of the following have been encountered in the span—general decomposition, either vegetative or corporeal, feces, or carbon emissions— purification is required. Discard clothing and proceed to—"

Eunice stepped back, riffling through the parchments on the door. Hundreds of detailed statutes specifying everything from the type of footwear allowed in Industry to unbecoming conduct once inside.

"This is… *impossible*." She gaped at Joseph. "I can't do all this. If I tried, I'd be here for days."

"You'd be here forever," Joseph said drolly. "Which is the point, I guess."

"So how'd my mother ever get in?"

"She didn't. But it wasn't for lack of trying."

"Next you're gonna tell me that the road to hell is paved with good intentions."

Joseph sighed.

"Okay," Eunice said. "So what are we gonna do?"

He looked steadfastly at her. "There's only one thing you can do."

The scroll of laws rustled dryly as a breeze swept past. Eunice had never been one for rules. Not that she was a rule-breaker. Compliance with a set of rules had not freed her from chemical addiction. Vows and pledges had been no substitute for simple surrender. She was powerless to heal herself—that's how the credo put it. And it was that admission that stripped the Law of its power. As long as these ridiculous decrees remained posted, her mother would remain bound.

Eunice stared at the scroll.

Then she marched over and snatched the parchments off the door. One by one, she ripped them in half, releasing them into the breeze. The sheets skittered across the earth, disappearing as they went. After the last page had completely vanished, Eunice stood listening to the lonely howl of the wind across the Plains of Cinder.

The door creaked open behind her.

She jumped at the sound, thinking that maybe the tower was collapsing. Mordant yammered something about heights and rites and transient delights. She ignored him, crept forward, and poked her head inside. The smell of must and mold was so strong that she staggered back, coughing.

Eunice flung her arm over her face and prepared to enter. As she did, the molten sun flumed on the horizon, rocking the earth. Mordant stumbled back blubbering as Eunice clung to the doorway. Chunks of plaster clattered to the earth around her. Suddenly, Joseph shoved her through the doorway as a block of mortar thumped the earth where she had been standing. The quake rolled to a stop. She had fallen inside the Tower of Industry and knelt as a cloud of dust settled around her.

And she was sure she had broken another nail.

Eunice bustled to her feet, choking against the grit. Joseph hurried inside, yanking Mordant through the narrow doorway.

"We have to hurry," Joseph said. "Your mother—" He glanced worriedly outside.

Eunice stared up into the heart of the structure. It was hollow, ribbed with beams and braces. A narrow stairwell followed the interior walls, rising precariously to a distant point up high above.

"He's up there," Eunice sighed, unable to keep herself from sounding disheartened. "All the way up there."

"C'mon!" Joseph summoned Mordant and marched to the steps. "We don't have time."

She nodded to herself and followed them. The stairs were unusually steep. From the size of them, Reverend Ash had to be ten feet tall. The higher they climbed, the more sheer the steps became. Mister Mordant took to slinging his arms over each step and hoisting himself over the edge, complaining between every exaggerated breath. Up above, a pale light grew and she could make out windows and a vast platform.

Eunice caught herself thinking about the scroll of laws she had destroyed. It wasn't the first time she had broken someone's rules. But she did not anticipate the guilt and fear that now possessed her as a result of that act. Whoever Reverend Ash was, he could rightly hold her to account. And she feared what that might entail.

The building seemed to sag under their weight, groaning as they ascended. By the time they reached the final platform, Eunice's mind was swirling. The stairway led to an iron-hinged hatch in a wooden floor. Joseph heaved the door open and it clanged on the other side. Then he hoisted himself up and reached down for Mordant.

"Can't climb! Mmph. Mordant can't climb." Yet despite his frantic dissent, Mordant took Joseph's hand.

Eunice positioned herself behind the grub, took a great breath, held it, and pushed Mordant over the ledge. He issued a yelp. Before following, she braced herself against the wall and looked down on the winding stairwell. She gasped. It looked as if they climbed miles. Miles! As if they were seated in the clouds atop Jack's beanstalk. They had climbed high… *but not this high!* She flattened her back against the wall. Her heart raced.

"I can go back," she said to herself. "Whenever I want. I can go back."

And then she thought about her mother laying in Saint Luke's dying of brain cancer. And if there was any way this was related to that, she could not give up. Not now.

"It always looks higher from up here." Joseph extended his hand, a knowing smile creasing his lips. "C'mon."

She found comfort in his presence. Eunice took his hand and he hoisted her through the trap door, where she collapsed on the landing.

Her head was spinning from the thinning oxygen. Or was it from the view? Or was it from the car accident she had been in on the 210 freeway? She only allowed herself a moment to speculate. Eunice bolted upright and began scanning the loft.

Threads of gray light shone through the cracks of a high-pitched, open beamed ceiling. The wind whistled through unseen apertures and, up here, the tower creaked terribly. Except for its perimeter, the room was empty and uncluttered. Tall thin windows rose every four or five feet. From this perch, one could probably get a 360-degree view of Winterland. Not that Eunice was dying to have a look. Up here, the slightest movement could be felt ten-fold. Every creak. Every groan. Every structural shift. If there was another solar flare, this place would become a pile of matchsticks.

"Egads!" someone shouted in a high-pitched warble. "What have you done?"

Eunice spun around, looking for the source of the airy voice.

"Industry is breached!" the voice twilled. "Profaned! Sullied by the unwashed. Curses!"

Eunice's gaze darted about the airy loft, but she could see no one.

"Heathens!" the voice cried. "Purification from the heathens!"

Then Eunice noticed that someone was standing... *in the rafters*. What in the world was this person doing? She forced her eyes to adjust, and took a step closer. It was a thin, terribly frail man with a pointy nose and a bulky device strapped to his head. But he wasn't standing in the rafters.

He was standing on stilts.

TEN

Joseph looked up at the stilted man. "Stop being so dramatic, Reverend."

"I have foreseen this." The reverend's voice was hollow, yet lilting, like the tinkling of wind chimes. "The end of all things."

"Not *all* things," Joseph said. "Just *your* things."

Reverend Ash adjusted the device on his head. It was an odd contraption, an oversized helmet consisting of mechanical arms with various lenses and monocles. His long bony fingers drew one spectacle back and swiveled a large eyeglass into its place. He calibrated the piece, stepped forward and teetered on his stilts, looking down upon Eunice through the thick lens.

"Her!" Ash gasped. "She has broken the Law!"

"Well I—" Eunice instinctively looked at her filthy hands, fearing the reverend might begin an inspection of her fingernails. Then she crossed her arms. "How could *anyone* keep those laws? They were… *impossible*."

"Impossible indeed!" Reverend Ash drew back the lens with his delicate fingers and straightened. "Only the blameless can satisfy the Law. Which is why I *alone* dwell in the Tower of Industry."

Eunice scowled. "I suppose that's why my mother never made it inside?"

"Your mother had her chance." Reverend Ash brushed his hand through the air dismissively. "Many are called but few are frozen."

"Don't you mean *chosen*?"

"Frozen, Spawn. *Frozen*." Ash maneuvered toward one of the windows where several telescopic devices stood in array looking down upon the Plains of Cinder.

The grub man mumbled something behind her. Eunice turned to see Mister Mordant sulking in the shadows.

"Safer with me," he groused. "Shoulda stayed with Mordant."

Reverend Ash spun about so quickly Eunice thought he might fall off his stilts. He thumped toward Mordant, navigating through the beams while fiddling with his monocles. Then he bent forward and gawked comically at the creature.

"Defiled!" Ash twilled, throwing his gangly arms up in dismay. "How dare you bring this worm into Industry!"

"Sorry, Reverend." Joseph wandered to one of the telescopes and looked through it. He said over his shoulder, "Industry's over."

"Pah!" Ash lurched toward Joseph, brushing him away from the telescope. Then he turned, teetered, and glared at them. "Industry stands forever! A monument to Diligence. Enterprise. Devotion." He allowed the last word to trail off rapturously.

Eunice watched him swaying there with his eyes closed in near euphoria. She cleared her throat. "A monument?" She let her gaze wander about the decrepit tower. "This thing's on the verge of collapsing."

Reverend Ash's brows creased, scrunching his already narrow face beyond recognition "Away with you!" he said, rushing at them on his stilts, waving his gangly arms like a manic scarecrow.

Mordant scuttled behind Eunice, snuffling and snorting. But she stood fast, gazing up at Reverend Ash. His bluster could not dissuade her... not after she had survived a car accident, a dimensional door, a crippled trekker, and the Swamp of Mlaise. She met the frenzied gaze of Reverend Ash.

Mordant seemed to derive courage from Eunice's resolve. He nudged from behind Eunice and said to Ash, "Comin' with us. Industry's over."

It was the first hint of glee Eunice had detected in the grub man's tone.

Reverend Ash sneered. "The Law requires no such thing." He rose tall on his stilts. "You must leave Industry at once! I must begin the Purification." His features relaxed into one of arrogant indifference.

Joseph crossed his arms and cast an expectant gaze at Eunice.

Eunice nodded to him—not at all confident, but understanding the laws of this strange dimension she had penetrated. She cleared her throat and looked up at the stilted man. "I don't know what you've done to my mother. But... it's over. She wants you. Both of you—" She pointed to Mordant and then Ash. "You're coming with us and... and there's no way you're gonna weasel your way out of it."

Reverend Ash appeared momentarily stunned. Perhaps he had never had a woman stand up to him. He cast a brief glance at Mordant, as if the grub man would rally to his side. "Pah!" he finally said. "I rescued her from this foul creature."

"Rescued?" Mordant protested. "Mmph! You stole her!" He stomped his foot for emphasis.

"She came willingly," Ash piped. "Who would not? You disgrace Industry with your lies."

"*Lies?*" Mister Mordant stumbled out from behind Eunice with his arms unfurled. "You're the one. It's your stupid Law—that's the lie!"

"The Law," Ash preened. "Yes. The Law says you must go. Article 8, Precept 17, Section C. Only the *Deserved* shall enter Industry. And you are *not*. So go!" He wiggled his long pale fingers toward the three of them. "Back the way you came, Spawn. Leave this holy place at once. The end of all things is at hand. I must prepare for Night, for the Coronation. She takes the throne, you know. And I shall be frozen, interminably ensconced in my citadel. Alas! The Purification must begin." He folded his hands at his waist and gazed smugly at them.

Mordant flashed a worried glance at Eunice, and then snuffled back into the shadows again.

Eunice glanced at Joseph who had moved back to the telescopes and was gazing out at the fiery horizon.

"The Law," Eunice said to herself. "You're bound to the Law."

"Of course!" Ash peeled. "It is what binds her world. Your mother put it in place and assigned *me* to guard it."

She peered up at him. "Well, then that's why she wants you."

"He's right." Joseph stepped back from the telescope and stood gaping. "The Coronation is beginning. If she's enthroned..." He looked steadfastly at her. "We have to leave."

"Indeed!" Reverend Ash rose imperiously. "You must leave. Go on, Spawn. You and your troupe. Your appeals are useless. You have no authority here."

Maybe he was right. What kind of authority could Eunice really have here? She could barely keep her life together. So how on earth did she expect to command a grub man and a stilted scarecrow through an unpredictable netherworld?

"Well, I'm h-here," Eunice began, trying to formulate the thoughts that were brewing inside her. "I-I'm here because she *gave* me authority. Or someone did. I have the authority to be here. I made him come with me." She pointed at Mordant. "And I led us out of that awful swamp. And I can go back whenever I want, right?" She nodded toward Joseph, who met her with an affirming wink. "I broke your Law—or *her* Law, like you said. And maybe that's what she wanted. I..." She forced down a swallow. "I tore it up."

"No!" Reverend Ash gasped and staggered back. His helmet slid down over his eyes, and he stood teetering on his rickety stilts, frantically trying to fit the device back into place. It rested cockeyed on his head. "No one can... You didn't!"

"I did."

Joseph made his way to the trap door and stood waiting for them.

"It was just some pieces of paper anyway," Eunice said. "They turned into nothing, just disappeared. Which is probably what they were all along. Nothing."

Ash gaped. Then his eyes darted about the spire sanctuary. "It's Sybil," he warbled. "She's the one."

"Who?"

"Eunice," Joseph urged. "We have to go."

"It's her fault," Ash thumped toward Eunice, his sanctimony suddenly as vapid as the laws it had been attached to. "Sybil went too far. Your mother would have been safe here. Sybil gave her too much. She always does." He tilted his helmet back and leaned forward. His eyes were rabid. "The Law would not have allowed this!"

"Well…" Eunice pursed her lips. "There's a new Law in town. It's me."

When she spoke this, an explosion sounded. The horizon flared and Industry rocked violently at the repercussion. Ash shrieked and staggered across the room trying to steady himself. He thudded against one of the beams and clung to it like a drowning man on a life preserver. The helmet fell from his head and shattered sending mirrors, springs, and thick lenses spiraling across the floor. The structural beams groaned and crackled as the tower swayed from one side to the other. Particles of plaster and dust rained down. Finally, everything settled. Only the moaning of the wind could be heard.

"It's the Coronation." Joseph said. "We gotta hurry."

Eunice herded Reverend Ash and Mister Mordant to the roof hatch. Mordant stood wringing his hands, while Ash wavered on his stilts, staring down into the bowels of his decrepit tower. He blurted, "Someone will answer for this!"

Eunice extended her hand to help him.

"Don't touch me." Ash wrinkled his nose at her and began to wobble his way down.

Mordant watched the gaunt stilted man descend the stairs and snuffled, "What goes up must come down."

ELEVEN

Their descent from the Tower of Industry was amazingly swift. In fact, once they reached the bottom, Eunice was forced to conclude she had misjudged its height completely. She stood outside and looked up in puzzlement at the tower.

"It looked a lot bigger on the inside," Eunice wondered aloud.

"Doesn't it always?" Joseph quipped.

Reverend Ash seemed to take great offense at this. But he had no retort. He wobbled to a standstill under the burnished sky, looking forlorn. Mister Mordant, however, appeared greatly relieved to be down from Industry. He began rooting around in the dry earth as if he were a pig in a sty, tossing clods of dirt on his head.

Suddenly the sky erupted overhead, crimson plumes radiating against a growing blackness. They all turned and stared. A sickening emptiness gripped Eunice for a monstrous chasm now appeared in the ozone, enveloping the periphery of her vision. A pitch starless sky, a great Nothingness. She tore her eyes away from the apocalyptic dreamscape.

"Okay." She swallowed. "So how do we get to this Sybil?"

Reverend Ash looked away from the savage sky and the door where the Law had been posted. His features were gaunt and drawn. He shook his head dejectedly, swaying in the breeze. "There is no one way. She has many ways. Many roads lead to her."

"So…" She craned up at him. "How do we find her?"

He straightened and trilled angrily, "Without the Law, there is nowhere else to go but to her. You should have thought about that before you destroyed the sacred texts." He jabbed his bony finger at the vacant door. Then he shook his head and said, "Now she is unfettered. And who knows what form she will take."

Eunice stared at him. A howl rose from the plain and the tower creaked behind her. The wind was growing chill and the damp smell of evening was in it.

"Then we'll follow the stream," Eunice said emphatically. "The stream will get us there."

Apparently, Joseph agreed. He was at her side in a moment and together they began marching down, past the ancient archway, into the Plains of Cinder.

Mordant moaned behind them and she could hear him heave his body from the dirt and begin plodding after them. Eunice did not need to turn to see if Ash was following. The laws of Winterland would not allow him to remain without her.

But she had yet to consider the consequences of this.

Sheets of sand swept across the highway, swallowing it completely in parts. The odd foursome passed the rusted shell of an automobile, partly buried in a dune. Its vanity license plate read R33LIST. Mordant saw it and scurried past, murmuring something about monsters. Soon after that, they encountered the ruins of a vast overpass. Its columns lay toppled like great petrified trees in a primeval world. The wind whistled through the rubble carrying the awful choir in its dry deathly current.

As they walked the Plains of Cinder, Eunice found herself wondering at her mother's journey. Perhaps that old proverb was true: Never judge a person until you walk a mile in their shoes. It left her feeling guilty for judging her mother. Eunice recalled her own journey out of addiction and how much it felt like a wasteland. Watching the carnage of her life—the squandered opportunities, the broken friendships, the wasted talents—was strangely similar to this surreal desert.

The sand eventually yielded to parched cracked earth and the black rivulet disappeared underground.

"It's gone!" Eunice lurched to a stop, hunched over the spot where the stream had vanished. "Dried up."

Joseph shook his head. "It never goes away. You should know that."

She looked sideways at him. "Is that another riddle?"

He cast a chiding glance at her.

She sighed. "I know—even the truth can sound like a riddle when you're on the wrong side of it."

They resumed walking. The Plains of Cinder was like a vast salt flat. Plates of earth warped by some great sun stretched for miles. The wind chilled her flesh, and she hugged herself, hoping for warmth. Yet Joseph seemed unfazed. He marched on in his steady, yet halted gait.

Finally, she asked, "Why do you limp, Joseph?"

"Because of what happened on the other side."

"You're from... *my side*?"

"Of course," he snorted. "Where else would I be from?"

"Of course." She stared forward. "So, what happened?"

"Hm," Joseph said contemplatively. "Let's say I had my own demons." He jabbed his thumb over his shoulder at the motley troupe bringing up the rear. "I surrendered to them and I'll bear the wound forever, just like Good bears the scar of Evil."

"So," Eunice said hesitantly, "are you an angel?"

"On, no. I'm what I always was, only more so."

She waited, but he did not offer clarification. And she knew that getting a clear answer would not be possible. So Eunice simply nodded to herself.

The landscape spread before them, cold and bleak. The sky grew darker, and the wind picked up, beating on them with rigid persistence. Soon Eunice's lips grew parched and she realized how thirsty she'd become. She was almost hoping a Mad Hatter would arrive with a cup of tea.

But she could not ask to stop. Instead, she turned her attention to Reverend Ash. His journey was particularly awful to watch. He clicked and clacked behind them, wobbling along, constantly on the verge of collapsing.

After witnessing his tortured march, Eunice gestured to Reverend Ash's stilts. "You'll move a lot faster if you get rid of those things."

"These *things* are my legs, Spawn."

"Kidding, right?"

He puffed in dismissal. "One does not *kid* about such matters." Then he looked away with an air of disregard.

"Okay," Eunice sighed. "I'm sorry."

"Indeed," he said dryly.

"It's just... you're not any bigger with those stilts on. You're the same size either way. Besides," she forced a smirk back. "They're pretty flimsy."

"This from a woman who relied on synthetics for the better part of her adult life."

"Hey."

"Not only that, but you abandoned your mother when she needed you most."

"That's not fair. And way too personal."

"Cht!" Ash thrust forth his hand to silence her. "Do what you must," he chimed. "You'll see. You should have left when you had a chance. Why meddle here? The Law has remained untouched... until *you* intruded." He pointed a dreadfully rigid finger at her. "Sybil will have her way. She will twist your mind and leave your carcass to waste in Winterland. The Coronation will ensue and you will become enshrined in her Garden. Another one of her many trophies. Testament to that flaccid apparatus you call," he drawled the phrase, "*your mind.*"

Eunice opened her mouth to speak, but found no retort. After fumbling about for one, she said, "You're mean."

"The truth hurts." Reverend Ash casually inspected his nails. "Or so I hear."

Eunice turned away from Reverend Ash and hurried to Joseph's side. But there was no consolation for her. Between Mordant and Ash, she could see why her mother had gone mad.

A growing dread of this person Sybil loomed on her mind. If she were to be stuck here, would she go insane? Even worse, would she be trapped in some type of hell?

They walked on. Her thirst became insatiable. Eunice licked her parched lips and fatigue tugged at her mind. The dry blasted Plain was wearing on her. Even summer in SoCal was better than this blighted interstate.

"Oh-h-h," Mordant cried out. "Not doing well. Mmph! Must rest."

She turned to see Mister Mordant plop onto the cracked earth and slump forward, blubbering.

"We'll never make it. Prt-fff!! Trials and torments. Misery's the lot. Aw!" Tears tumbled from his face, splashing on the hard dirt. "Doomed, we are! All doomed."

Eunice came to a stop, as did Reverend Ash, who rolled his large eyes at the pathetic creature. But watching Mordant slumped there seemed to magnify Eunice's own exhaustion.

"He's right," she said. "We should sit down. Just for a minute."

And before she knew it, Eunice was sitting cross-legged on the ground across from Mister Mordant. He dabbed the tears from his eyes and snuffled his approval.

"I'm so thirsty," she said, brushing the hair from her face. "And tired too."

"Thirsty, yes," Mordant said. "Cinder does that. See? The pretties need rest. Mmmph! Hard, I tell ya. The stew needs stirrin'. And the rot—oomph! Better to burrow."

"You shut up!" Eunice shot an angry glare at Mordant. "I'm not listening to you anymore."

"Rt! Not listening to your old friend?"

"We aren't friends." Eunice yawned. "Remember?"

A great wave of exhaustion seemed to be upon her. She groggily turned toward the Plains of Cinder to see Joseph standing some distance away, silhouetted against the angry sky. She wanted to call out, but thought it best to conserve her energy. He would wait for her. She just needed to close her eyes.

"So tired," she slurred, and lay back on the ground. "Just a minute. Tell him… to wait."

She could hear Mister Mordant speaking, but he seemed to be far away.

"…ret inside… mergen… un…"

Those words…

"to the… over aw… stit…"

And then came the smell of exhaust fumes and burning rubber.

It was never far away—isn't that what Joseph said? But if she left now, what would happen to her mother? Eunice had promised to fight. But matches like this never ended in a draw.

She tried to open her mouth to speak, to shake herself from the malaise. But a deathly cold seemed to drape her.

"The four of us." It was Mordant's voice. "Together. Mmph! We can sleep here. A *long* sleep. Then we'll never have to be alone."

She nodded to herself. *Sleep*. They'd walked for miles and seemed no closer to her destination than when she'd left. Besides, if this were all a dream, then she would wake up on the other side of this with only a vague recollection of Winterland and its bizarre inhabitants. That wouldn't be all that bad.

Eunice groaned. A chill swept by and she shivered. She was tumbling into the restful dark. Where people were waiting for her.

When she was a child, sleep had been a way of escape—escape from her parents' divorce, escape from her mother's prostitution. Escape from her abandonment. Perhaps this was why so many fairy creatures came out at night. Peter Pan. The fae. Goblins and ghoulies. Sleep was their playground, and now they were coming out to play.

"Eunice…"

The voice was distant. Maybe it was Granny Em, summoning Eunice back to the cottage of misery.

"Eunice…"

Perhaps it was her father. How long had it been since she'd heard him? Did he know how much pain he had caused her? Did he realize he'd short-circuited her adolescence and forced her to grow up?

"Eunice…"

Then again, maybe it was the Lexus man, calling her back into the land of the living where a freeway full of pissed off commuters were waiting for her. Her playtime was over and now it was time to go and face the stark realities of her life.

"Eunice!"

She awoke with a start. A dark shape was huddled over her with sickly red eyes, full of hate and hunger. Rank breath pelted her and on it was blood and death. She gasped for breath, but the air had been sucked out of her lungs. No! She couldn't die here.

Eunice forced out a scream and scrambled to her feet, flailing at the dark shape huddled over her.

But no one was there.

Reverend Ash stood alone, some distance away, picking at particles on his clothing, while Mordant had managed to scratch out a hovel and lay squatted inside it. They both gawked at her.

She gripped her throat just to make sure the deathly dream presence had not remained.

Joseph stood on an escarpment looking out on the barren plain. But something had changed. Something about the smell and lay of the land was different. He turned and anxiously waved her forward. Eunice glanced at Ash and Mordant, recalling her claustrophobic nightmare. She walked toward Joseph, peering at the changing topography. And what she saw stopped her in her tracks.

A war zone spread before her.

Craters marred the landscape, bomb-blasted cavities that sent threads of smoke writhing skyward. Behind them laid an enormous ribbed structure silhouetted against the awful sky. And Eunice stood gaping at what looked like the hull of a massive structure collapsed on the tarmac.

It was the remains of a blimp.

TWELVE

"Blimps weren't exactly my thing," said Eunice absently. "Or my mother's."

"They don't have to be," Joseph said. "Just part of the psychography. Got dropped into the subconscious somewhere along the way, took root and fermented. Random firings, maybe. Either way, it's there so… C'mon."

Then he lurched onto the highway, limping straight for the cyclopean dirigible.

"But what does it mean?" Eunice called after him.

He didn't stop to respond.

The wind picked up, whipping her hair about her face. The red sky was now a nuclear copper, weaving threads into the inky black sky. Dante's choir had resumed its hellish cantata, a macabre soundtrack to the proceedings.

"It's her," a voice gasped at her elbow.

Eunice spun to see Mister Mordant at her side, biting his nails, staring wide-eyed at the war zone before them.

"What an ungodly habitat," Reverend Ash droned from the other side.

"What?" she said. "Who?"

"Sybil. Br-r-r." Mordant shook his jowls. "I knew it. She's havin' us for dinner. Aw-w! Misery, woe, stitched for travel! Pllt! Playthings on a sinkin' ship—that's all we are!"

"Dinner?!" Eunice swallowed. "But I'm not hungry."

Reverend Ash lifted his chin. "I go to my death with dignity. Stay behind if you must, Spawn." He lurched forward.

Mordant muttered something, threw his hands in the air, and burst after Reverend Ash with a frothy cry.

Eunice remained, watching the three of them descend toward the blimp. "Fight," she said to herself, trying to be convincing. "You gotta fight." Then Eunice hurried after them.

The terrain grew more blasted and treacherous as she went. Piles of smoking debris glowed here and there. They passed the fuselage of a plane and shards of shrapnel. She even glimpsed the barrel of a canon protruding from an ash heap. The 210 had seen its share of road rage and fender benders, but Eunice could not recall a civil war having been waged here. Yet if this was her mother's world, civil wars were probably a regular occurrence.

She maneuvered her way through a series of potholes and small crevices and joined Joseph.

He glanced at her. "Lovely, isn't it?"

"My mother lives..." Eunice stared up at the gargantuan blimp, "*here?*"

"Your mother? No. It's Sybil. Reverend Ash was right about one thing—without the Law, she's got more room. And apparently, firepower. Whatever you do," Joseph said, "stay on your toes. Okay? She's slippery."

The red, hate-filled eyes she'd encountered in her dream hovered in her mind. Eunice forced the vision out of her head. She licked her parched lips, and then nodded.

Mounds of gravel and tarmac, upturned by some cataclysm, opened along the way like huge abscesses in the highway. The closer they got to the ribbed structure, the more Eunice began to approximate its size. Massive curved planks rose into the sky like the scaffolding of an ancient coliseum. It was far bigger than any dirigible she had ever seen. Thirty, maybe forty stories high. It stretched across the entire highway, its nose collapsed into the earth. Tattered skin draped its framework, flapping in the breeze like banners from a bygone crusade.

They passed a smoldering crater. Then another. Finally, Joseph trudged onto the rim of one and stared down into it. "Eunice," he called. "You should see this."

"Ohhp!" Mordant yelped. Then he pressed his finger to his lips. "Shhh! Monsters. We don't wanna waken the monsters."

Monsters? Eunice gazed at him.

"You pathetic worm!" Ash stared down his nose at Mordant. "The only monsters are the ones in your head. Superstitious twit!" He spotted soot on his shoulder and quickly brushed it off.

Joseph continued to motion her forward.

She looked from Ash to Mordant, and then climbed up and stood on the edge of the steaming pit.

Embers crackled inside and the soil revealed strata embedded with unusual shapes and fragments. Something had been unearthed by these blasts. She covered her nose and bent at the waist, trying to identify the puzzle of objects entombed in that blackened earth. An ivory tusk. A breastplate with ornate carving. A fair winged nymph lying in a fetal position. Eunice gasped and rose slowly. The entire crater was lined with fossils and artifacts. She was walking across the graveyard of some rich, fantastical world.

"What is it?" Eunice said. "It's beautiful."

And indeed it was. Precious stones glinted in the light, jade and jasper, amethyst and ruby, strewn amidst other treasures. It was as if some splendid antediluvian world had undergone the wrath of Vesuvius. This was once her mother's world, a rich subliminal gallery now blasted from her mind by madness. Angels, fairies, valiant warriors, and maidens, torpedoed and left to ferment under this hellish sky.

Eunice could not help but feel they were on holy ground.

She brushed a tear from her cheek. What could have caused this? What monstrous thing would have—?

"Look!" Mordant cried.

His cry tore Eunice from her euphoria. She turned to see a child, slight and nimble, running through the debris field.

"It's her!" Joseph navigated his way down the crater, fumbling for Eunice's hand as he went.

"Her who?"

"Sybil!" He yanked her forward. "She's the last one. The strongest of all three."

"I beg pardon." Ash looked haughtily at Joseph.

"Did she do this?" Eunice pointed at the crater. "Did she destroy those... *things*?"

Joseph turned and looked at her. "Those things can't be destroyed. Buried? Yes. But it seems like this war, and whoever waged it, might have accidentally jogged her memory. C'mon."

Joseph hurried after the child, dodging shrapnel and glowing pits. Eunice was at his heels, her mind going a hundred miles an hour. What other wonders lay just below the great highway? But she didn't have time to speculate. They entered the blimp, passing through two massive joists that formed an archway. Before she knew it, they had entered a wall of bushes. Tall, thorny brambles rose on each side of them. They were on a trail, zig-zagging through a vast maze of shrubbery. The bushes blocked out everything but the tumultuous sky overhead.

This child was leading them through a maze.

Or into one.

"We're gonna get lost," she called to Joseph. "Be careful."

Left turn. Right. Another right. Then a long corridor with multiple adjoining branches. The child stopped and turned, daintily brushing down her dress. She was a nymph-like figure, with skin so fair and white it might have been porcelain. She met Eunice's eyes and giggled, before playfully bolting into another row of brambles.

Ash and Mordant barreled from the hedges behind them and skidded to a stop just as Joseph and Eunice went the opposite direction after the little girl.

"Wait for me!" Mordant yelped. "Ain't made for bushies!"

Their trek through the bramble maze was dizzying. Eunice's arms were scratched and her clothing was tattered by the prickly limbs. The exhaustion seized upon her again. She couldn't go on much longer at this pace. In fact, curling up for a nap seemed altogether reasonable. Just as she was about to tell Joseph to stop, they turned a corner and tumbled into a grassy clearing.

The Garden of Eden spread before them.

Eunice sat up, awestruck. A lush carpet of green descended to a crystalline pond. The scent of fresh spring grass reawakened senses she thought had been cauterized by this viscous world. Was she even breathing? For a moment, she forgot everything, entranced by this Shangri-La inside the ruined blimp. Eunice brushed her fingers through the grass, drawing in its scent. It was like a revelation! How could it be? She rolled onto her back doing snow angels on the lawn.

Mordant and Ash stood over her, gaping in astonishment.

Overhead, the framework of the fallen blimp formed a massive dome. From its planks and beams hung lush plants and flowering vines. Eunice sat up to take in this astounding new world, for the biggest surprise of all awaited her: a spire of rock from which tumbled a gurgling fountain. At its base, white swans lazed amidst lily pads and dragonflies zipped through smooth boulders. Seated atop one of these boulders sat Sybil.

Eunice scrambled to her feet, trying shake off the intoxication of the scene.

Sybil spotted her and waved. "I'm glad you came. Come look!" She pointed excitedly into the pond.

As Eunice stepped forward, Joseph put his hand on her arm. "She has to come, Eunice. It's the only way."

Eunice nodded dimly, remaining fixed on the porcelain princess. Before she knew it, she had brushed Joseph aside and began walking along the lawn to the child.

Sybil smiled as Eunice approached. "They told me you were coming."

"Who?"

The girl smiled and pointed into the pond.

A school of large red goldfish lolled below the surface, looking as if they were waiting to be fed.

Eunice turned back to the child. Her complexion was flawless and she exuded an aura of innocence. Who could this little one be? Out here in Nowhere Land.

Eunice squinted at her. "The *goldfish* told you I was coming?"

Sybil giggled. "No, silly. They did." She pointed to Joseph, Mordant and Ash, who stood at a distance, watching their exchange.

Eunice drew up her courage. "Then you know I'm coming to take you back to my mother."

"Oh my dear." Sybil placed her hand over her mouth. "Then they haven't told you."

"Told me what?" Eunice asked skeptically.

The little girl gazed at Eunice. "You died in that car accident."

THIRTEEN

Eunice swayed, then steadied herself and refocused on Sybil. This would explain everything. Eunice *had* died in the car accident! How else could such a vivid world and such exotic, terrifying fauna, be possible? And seem so real? It was real! But if she was dead, where was she? Perhaps this wasn't a test about her mother at all. She had died and was passing to heaven. All that stuff about traveling through a tunnel of light was wrong.

Then again, maybe all this proved was that even after death, she could still over-think things.

Joseph approached. "You've done enough damage, Sybil."

"Me?" Sybil said to Joseph. "Why, you haven't even told her the truth."

"What haven't you told me?" Eunice said to Joseph, with far too much suspicion in her tone. "Are you keeping something from me?"

Joseph peered at Sybil, and appeared to be mulling something. "You're right. Maybe it *is* time I told her the truth." He turned to Eunice. "Your mother has nurtured three spirits. Sybil's one of them. They are parasites, consuls of hell—all of them, concerned with only one thing: maintaining real estate. They've been passed down through your family for generations. Well, when you went to rehab, you interrupted the food chain. And they don't like you. They never liked you. But now it's an issue of survival—theirs or yours. So don't let them fool you with their looks," he gestured to Sybil, "or their words. Because if you don't destroy them, your mother will be crowned Queen of Winterland. And their circle will remain... unbroken."

Sybil slipped off the rock and ambled to the pond, apparently unconcerned about Joseph's indictment. She began gathering wildflowers from amidst the boulders, bundling them into a colorful bouquet.

Eunice looked from Joseph to Sybil, and back. "Then I didn't die in that accident?"

"No," Joseph said flatly. "But if you get stuck here, then all bets are off." He shrugged. "I told you there was risk involved."

"Generational spirits?" Eunice said to no one.

Joseph nodded. "Think of it as your spiritual gene pool."

"I'd rather not. And that part about going back whenever I want?"

"You still can," Joseph said. "But if you do, they win."

"Go back?" Sybil straightened. "Why would you want to do that? Just look." She lifted her hands and twirled through the grass. "It's like paradise here."

Eunice stared at the little girl. Even though it was an illusion, Eunice could not deny the beauty of this place. Especially after trudging through Mlaise and the Plains of Cinder. Just because it was a *virtual* world did not make it any less beautiful. Right? However, if they really wanted her to leave, as Joseph suggested, why did Sybil object? Why would the little girl—or the *generational spirit*—want Eunice to stay? Perhaps she was playing a trick on Eunice, reverse psychology. Then again, maybe Joseph was conspiring with the three of them.

Exhaustion and its accompanying thirst bore down on her again. She drew a deep breath and slumped onto the grass with a great sigh. Eunice sat there massaging her temples.

Sybil stopped picking the flowers and looked out of the corner of her eye at Eunice.

Your spiritual gene pool. If there was such a thing, Eunice's was probably more like a toxic waste dump. She shook her head. Was it possible to even fight such a thing? Battling ones' biology was like shadow boxing—there was never a winner. Unless the shadow was counted as a real opponent.

But the idea of surrender wasn't in her nature either. Thank God.

Suddenly something flashed. The entire sky erupted, as if some great device had been detonated on the horizon. And behind it rolled a massive quake. The earth rippled, heaved and buckled. Mordant shrieked, claiming this was the end, while Reverend Ash teetered wildly on his stilts, professing his virtue. Planks of wood sheared away from the dirigible overhead and clattered to the ground. A cataract began churning in the pond as several boulders split in two.

Sybil ran to Eunice. "Make it stop! Please!"

"Me?" Eunice cried, bracing herself against the concussions. "What did I do?"

Sybil dropped her bouquet and knelt down, fixated upon Eunice. "Don't you know why I'm here?"

Another blast rocked the earth.

"I—" Eunice glanced frantically at Joseph. "I'm not sure."

"My daddy left me here," Sybil said. "And my mother—she went to a bad place and couldn't take me with her."

Eunice peered at the girl. "They left you?"

"I know!"

"Out here?" Eunice glanced into the ashen sky.

Sybil nodded.

The tremors finally stopped. Dust clouds hung thick in the air. Eunice gazed upon the fair-skinned child. Smooth cheekbones and delicate lips. Eyes, dark and fathomless, like gemstone against ivory. This little girl looked so familiar.

"Who are you?" Eunice asked.

Sybil tilted her head, a coy smile curling the edges of her lips. "You don't know?"

Eunice shook her head, a sense of dread rising inside her.

"She left us here," Sybil said.

"She?"

"Our mother." Sybil stood, brushing the grass off her knees.

"What?"

"Our mother. I'm you, Eunice."

The words entered Eunice's mind like an adamantine spike. She was going insane; there was no other explanation. She stood gaping.

Finally, she glanced wordlessly at Joseph. He was watching with the utmost curiosity.

"I'm you, Eunice." Sybil giggled, spinning playfully in the grass. "It's how she wanted us to be. Innocent. Free. And the best playground ever! She never wanted to drag us through all that." Sybil spread her arms, motioning to the awful skyline outside the hull of the massive blimp. "That's why I'm here. She made a place just for me. It saved her, you know. It saved *us*. It was her gift, Eunice." Then Sybil lowered her head and her tone grew cold. "If you destroy me, you destroy her. Don't you know?"

Eunice peered at the girl.

Behind Eunice, Mordant prattled on about the ozone holes and skin cancer. Reverend Ash had retreated to the hedges, where he stood inspecting his clothing, his face pinched in disgust.

But something inside her hedged at Sybil's words.

Eunice would give anything for childlike innocence. She'd been forced to grow up way too fast, and then spent the rest of her life trying to recapture that lost childhood. Didn't everyone do that? Yet despite the glorious Eden that now spread before her, Sybil's words seemed hollow. Perhaps Joseph's warning had predisposed her toward suspicion. Perhaps Winterland had simply left its bitter mark on her, turned her cynical. Either way, not moving forward seemed like a greater crime than forcing this child-creature to take a hike.

Eunice swallowed hard and looked at the little girl. "You m-might have been me. A long time ago. You might even be what my mother *wanted* me to be, how she wanted to remember me. But you're n-not me, Sybil. Not the way I really am. Not now."

Sybil gaped and her countenance darkened.

An unexpected tone of empathy laced Eunice's words. "Mother'd like to remember me this way, I have no doubts. She never liked what I'd become. Which is why I'm so surprised she even invited me here. But if I'm not mistaken, that's what she wants to kill—this image of me, this part of her that's holding onto the past."

The sky seemed to deepen several shades. The clouds roiled overhead, as if some great dragon had been awakened, bringing with it a chill wet wind.

Eunice brushed the hair out of her face. "I came here to free my mother, Sybil. That's why I've put up with Mordant and Ash, and walked through that stupid swamp. That's what I conceded to do. And that's what I'm *gonna* do. I've spent enough of my life giving in to… to things I shouldn't. Things that *felt* good or *seemed* right. Running from crap instead of confronting it. But it never helped. I can't keep making that mistake." Eunice cast a sad smile at Sybil.

But the girl did not reciprocate the gesture. In fact, Sybil's features tightened, her eyes grew overshadowed and smoky.

Eunice stepped back so she could see her entire party. "The three of you—you're coming with us. I-I don't know what you did to my mother. Who you really are or what all this means. But she's at the end—I know that. And I'm… tired."

She looked to Joseph for confirmation. As she did, a brittle crackling filled the air. At first, Eunice could not tell what was happening. The atmosphere, the landscape—

everything seemed to be dying. The bouquet of flowers withered. The bright grass, the lily pads, the willows, the leaves—curled and shriveled before her eyes. Like a time-lapse photograph unreeling around them, she watched as the mirage that was the Garden of Eden, turned dead and gray. The pond began draining into sluice, leaving the goldfish flopping helplessly. Soon, everything was dry and blighted.

"Inevitable." Mordant whimpered. "It was inevitable."

Reverend Ash straightened, looking smug. "Perhaps if you had done your job, we wouldn't be here."

"Brr—rph!" Mordant snuffled. "Can't stop the rot. Tangles and prickles and beasties with sickles."

"There's laws for these things," Ash twilled. "But how would you know, you bleating bog of despair. If only you'd—"

"Shut up!" Sybil's eyes were like storm clouds, the veins in her temple throbbed. "This isn't over. There's someone else."

"Who?" Eunice looked at the girl. "What're you talking about?"

"Eunice!" Joseph called.

She tore her gaze away from the now mischievous-looking child, to Joseph. He pointed to the sky. The harpies were circling overhead like dark vultures.

"We have to hurry." Joseph turned toward the bramble maze. "C'mon!"

How would they ever make it back through the bushy labyrinth? All those twists and turns. It would take hours to find their way out. She turned to Sybil, who smiled wickedly.

"Mother told me to stay, Eunice." Sybil giggled. "And we shouldn't disobey mother, should we?"

Eunice glanced at Joseph who stood waiting at the entry to the brambles. Then she gazed up into the sky at the flying sentries. Apparently, whoever was waiting for her, knew she was close.

Eunice had never been the greatest with kids, which made it easier to grab Sybil by the hand and yank her forward.

"If you are me," Eunice said through gritted teeth, "it's time to grow up. If you're not me, then you have no business being in my mother's brain."

And with that she pulled the little girl toward the bramble maze, and its dark, glistening thorns.

FOURTEEN

Above them, the sky had turned cyclonic, whipping the brambles across their path like monstrous claws. Joseph led the way, but his steps grew more and more tempered. Great! She'd come all this way only to be trapped inside a prickly puzzle.

Sybil shuffled ahead of her, stubborn and withdrawn, not at all cooperative. Was Eunice this bratty as a child? If so, a good spanking seemed appropriate. Sybil's resistance forced Eunice to nudge the girl forward every few steps, turning their trek into a tug of war.

"Ooch!" Mordant yelped. "Ouchy!"

Reverend Ash, on the other hand, seemed to revel in the lashing. He spread out his arms allowing the thorny branches to strike him. "Such is the lot of all Good," he pronounced with sanctimony, wincing as he went.

The hedges seemed to grow higher and higher, tearing at her skin, leaving her clothing shredded and bloody. The harpies were gone and the hellish choir had resumed, serenading the sunset. Wispy flame-red tentacles faded against the cold black sky. It was almost night!

Suddenly, Joseph came to a stop at an intersection. His gaze wandered, forlorn, from one path to the next.

"Joseph!" Eunice shoved Sybil forward. "What's wrong?"

He shook his head, looking lost.

"She said there's someone else." Eunice stood beside him, panting. "I thought you said Sybil was the last one."

Joseph studied the thick bushes. "This is… new. It just happened. I can't see any further. Eunice." He turned toward her. "You're the only one who can do this."

"Huh?"

"Lost!" Mordant wailed. "Couldn't end good. Mmph! Never does. Never does."

Sybil laughed, a guttural, very un-childlike sound. "I told you we were supposed to stay. It's what she wants."

Eunice peered at the girl.

"It's punishment," Sybil said, raising her hands to the sky. "Can't you see? He tricked you." Sybil pointed an accusatory finger at Joseph. "The bent man is crooked inside. Now you've angered her, Eunice. And she's…" Her eyes narrowed. "She's strong now."

Eunice drew back.

"If you don't believe me," Sybil pleaded, "just turn around. Go back! You'll see. It'll stop."

A burst of wind sent dry leaves whirling around them.

Sybil's fair skin grew pallid and her eyes were becoming sunken pockets of night. Her dress was ragged at the edges and wafted about her like a spectral fog.

"Please," Sybil said, reaching toward Eunice. "You can stop it!"

Eunice brushed past the girl and stood in the intersection. Darkness swallowed the way before them. She gazed helplessly down the shadowed pathways. The scratching of the thickets and thorns made the bushes seem alive, heightening her distress.

Eunice did a 360 in the intersection, looking from one aisle to the next. But she was unable to discern which way they should go. Mordant whimpered, Ash crossed his arms and looked down his nose at her, while Sybil's mischievous smile returned.

Maybe Mordant was right; they were just playthings on a sinking ship, pawns to be sacrificed at the whim of some malicious deity. It's why her mother had cancer and Eunice got in a car accident on the way to the hospital. It was just one grand game of Hangman, with the human race always on the noose's end.

What an idiot! Now she was sounding like Mister Mordant.

Eunice looked up, past the hedges, into the sky.

And that's when she heard a faint trickle. Distinct from the dry rustle of the bushes. A thick watery sound ambling through the undergrowth.

"This isn't the way," Eunice said, now peering into the hedges. "The path is a trick. It's the stream—that's what we should follow."

She took a few steps, cocking her head toward the bramble. Then she poked her head through a nearby thicket of branches and remained there until her eyes adjusted.

Deep at the roots of the jungle, the black stream shimmered.

"I found it!" Eunice blurted. "C'mon!"

She parted the bushes for them.

"In there?" Mordant squalled. "Aw-w-w. Ain't made for bushies."

"Of course!" Joseph declared, before ducking under her arms into the net of scrub.

Reverend Ash looked sideways at her. "I suppose you consider this groveling?"

"What goes up," Eunice said, "must come down."

"Pah!" Ash snapped. Then he stooped at the waist and awkwardly made his way into the bushes. Mordant followed, leaving Sybil staring up at Eunice.

"It doesn't change anything, Eunice."

"I'm not listening to you."

"There's a monster you're missing." A wicked smile crept across Sybil's face. "It's always like that with you."

Eunice stared.

"You know what I mean," Sybil said. "You underestimate things. You always have. Just because you can forget about something and get on with your life doesn't mean it's done with. It's a fatal flaw, you know. They say everyone has one. Well, you have a blind spot for monsters."

The words stirred an ominous expectancy inside Eunice. Yes, she'd missed a lot of monsters. Drawing truces when she should have been kicking ass. Fleeing when she should have stood fighting. There was no shortage of second-guessing on her part. Still, she'd made her mind up.

In the end, the fatigue may have played part. Whatever the case, Eunice managed to gulp down her trepidation. "It's no worse than the other monsters I've already dealt with. And if they *are* worse, I'll deal with them too."

Sybil scowled. Then she girded up her dress and barreled into the bush.

Joseph led the way deep inside the bushy maze, snapping off branches as they went. They ducked and squeezed through the thorny bramble, following the black stream on its winding course. Occasionally, one of them would cry out after being pricked or scratched. Above them, outside the canopy of hedges, the storm increased. Thunder clapped, temporarily overriding the hellish choir, and the forest of brambles swayed. But the stream trudged onward.

Finally, they burst out the other side of the hedges and fell to the ground, choking and rubbing at their cuts.

"No more!" Mordant pleaded. "Blisters 'n rickets. Brr—rrph!"

Eunice lay panting, staring up at the viscous sky.

The earth was hard here. And there were sounds— something other than the wind and the cacophony of voices. It was a great hollow gasp, an inhalation, as if the entire world were drawing its final breath. She hoisted her body upward and turned toward the sound.

And what she saw snatched her breath from her lungs.

They had reached the end of the road.

The infernal hole in the sky had become a vortex of crackling ash. It was right on top of them, consuming her entire field of vision. The highway narrowed, funneling everything towards this horizon. Oily vines scrabbled along the perimeter, choking the guardrails and collapsed billboards like immense tumors along a metallic skeleton.

The black stream cut a line down the asphalt toward a vast canyon. A suspension bridge draped across this chasm, and a dark monstrous figure squat there, guarding the bridge.

And Eunice knew it was waiting for her.

FIFTEEN

It was black and angular, the size of a house, and when it saw them, it drew a great breath and roared. What emerged was a tumult of fierce, shrill cries, as if ages of woe were locked inside this being. Mordant fell to his knees at the sound, bawling, while Eunice clapped her hands over her ears and staggered backwards.

But she could not stifle its sound. Nor the pain it inflicted.

What a fool to think she could traverse someone's soul. Especially someone as screwed up as her mother. This was forbidden territory. She should have known that. You can't just waltz into someone's psyche and expect a tea party. Besides, her mother probably deserved this anyway—this hell. And Eunice deserved to live with the emptiness, the shadow of what could have been.

"Stop it!"

Joseph was shouting to her. But why bother?

"It's not you. Eunice!"

She removed her hands and turned to him, squinting against the gale.

"You can do it, Eunice," he implored. "You can finish this!"

She looked at the raging black beast and shook her head "Maybe we deserve it."

"Maybe. But it's not over yet!"

She nodded dumbly.

"You've done it before!" Joseph cried.

"Did I?"

"Yes!"

The monstrosity howled again and all of Winterland seemed to resonate with its pain. The creature's agony was embedded in the very fabric of this world. And its pain found resonance inside her. For Eunice knew this would have never happened, this foul inner world would have had no chance, if she would have just been more gracious, more forgiving. As it was, she'd allowed a monster to be borne inside her mother. A demon of hell that would never relent. She'd left her mother when it mattered most. Eunice rarely cut her slack and when she did, was quick to take it back. Mordant and Ash were as much Eunice's offspring as her mother's.

"Stop it!"

The voice was at odds with the awful choir.

"I said, *stop it*!"

Suddenly, she realized she was doubled over with her hands gripping her head. She straightened and looked at Joseph. Then she turned to the monster hunkered at the bridge. Exhaustion cumbered every iota of her being. She *so* wanted to be done with this, to silence the hellbeast. To bring peace to this savage world.

"What do I do?"

"Complete the bridge!" he shouted above the din.

She stared at Joseph, and then slumped forward. Did it have to be another riddle?

"Eunice!" He gripped both of her arms and demanded her attention. "You've gotta complete the bridge!"

Behind them, the bramble hedges rose like the Great Wall of China, dark and menacing. She had nowhere else to go but forward. Or go home. *If you can get to the end of this highway*, Joseph had said, *my riddles will make perfectly good sense.*

So it came down to trusting a gimpy trekker in a dream world.

She straightened and stared at Joseph.

"I've done this before, huh?"

"Yes!" Joseph laughed.

"Okay," she said to herself. "You haven't failed me yet."

Eunice turned toward the chasm.

90

A tempest burst around them, the storm becoming a tumult. Eunice's knees nearly buckled. The hole in the sky now towered overhead, ten times bigger than before, a gaping celestial lesion swirling debris, ringed with fiery teeth. Wind tore over its rim, sucking smoke and flame into the void. The menagerie of voices filled the air.

Eunice Ames shouted into the storm and hurtled herself forward, defiant.

How long that journey took, she could not say. It was if some cognitive expanse were being traversed, a circuit through a season or a mode of being rather than any real highway in a physical world.

Each step became heavier, burdening her with some new grief. The hellish cries awakened other voices inside her, voices from long ago. Demons she'd fought. Hungers she'd quelled. Like a scab torn free, the old wounds began oozing. The self-hatred that drove her into addiction, the loneliness and rejection that kept her there, the cheap, tawdry self-image rooted in her soul. She remembered the cold awareness that suicide ran in her veins and that her mother's minstrel spirit haunted the corridors of her mind. Every step closer to the dark thing seemed to open another petal on a diseased vine that had strangled Eunice's soul.

Yet she managed to trudge forward.

Which she also may have been genetically predisposed towards.

The monster had squared its body, preparing for their approach. The harpies stood sentry at its side, like palace guards in a Dali-esque abstract. Their owlish eyes followed her. Behind them, the suspension bridge rocked precariously over a vast dark chasm.

Complete the bridge.

Actually, she was surprised any bridges were left in her mother's world. Which was another reason to struggle onward.

The monster roared again and the black sun yawned. Now she could see the beast clearly. Its body was oblique, craggy, as if it had been hewn from the depths of some cursed mountain. It hunkered before the bridge, an impassable presence. Sunken inside its black frame were two red eyes— cold, merciless, hate-filled eyes—glaring at her from a faceless pit. It was searching, probing, stirring the cauldron of pain and self-pity inside her...

...pain and self-pity she thought she'd banished long ago.

But Eunice resisted the urge to flee, to turn away. It was one of the advantages of having already looked into the face of hell.

She stopped perhaps twenty feet from the hideous creature. Her hair whipped about her face. She fought to steady herself and stood tilted against the wind, staring into those abominable eyes.

Joseph was right—she'd fought this thing before.

Her company lumbered forward and stood beside her.

"See what you've made?" Sybil shouted, looking sideways at her.

"I'm not listening to you!"

"Apollyon!" Sybil cackled. "You can't let it go."

"*Apollyon?*" Eunice scowled. "What're you talking about?" Ignoring the little girl, Eunice turned to Joseph. "The bridge—how do we cross it?"

"We don't!"

She peered at him. "What?"

Joseph pointed at the beast, his hair whipping about his face. "You *complete* it."

"*Comple*—" Eunice pursed her lips. Then she yelled, "Would you stop playing games! What do I do?"

Joseph shook his head. "It came from the Abyss! It always does."

"So whaddo I do?!" she said through clenched teeth.

"Regret!" Joseph's voice was barely audible through the maelstrom. "It's regret!"

"It's a monster!"

"What else would it be?"

Eunice stood leaning against the wind. The thought disarmed her. So she turned and gaped at the demon.

Regret. Of course! If Mordant, Ash, and Sybil were incarnations of her mother's psyche, why not Regret? But perhaps even more enthralling than this realization was the notion that an abyss existed inside her mother's soul. It made Eunice wonder whether one could be found inside herself.

"So how do I get rid of it?" she yelled. "It's hers! She's gotta give it up!"

Joseph looked at her, and then slowly, knowingly, shook his head.

What was he saying?

"Eunice," Joseph said, "it yours!"

"Huh?"

He nodded. "You brought it along with you!"

Eunice's heart seemed to dull to a thudding standstill.

"*My* regret?" she said to herself. "It can't... This is mine?"

"How do you think you got here?" He stepped closer. "It's the bridge that binds both of you."

She looked at the monster. Its burning, hateful eyes were locked on her. Foam and spittle burst from its mouth as it bellowed. And the dreaded lamentation unraveled inside her. *How could this be?*

"I'm keeping us from going any further." The words seemed to fall out of her mouth. "I'm keeping *her* from going any further."

It was a confession, something that had been there along, just waiting to be voiced.

Some people nurture such things, she thought. Where else would regret rise but from some damnable place inside ones' psyche? But if anyone saw this monstrosity, they'd probably have second thoughts about coddling such emotions. However, other than her admission, how exactly did one relinquish a demon the size of a tour bus? Especially when it was birthed from their own anguish?

The beast stomped and released a howl, and the fiery sky above it whirled. The confluence of devilish voices rose. Yet knowing what this thing was suddenly seemed far more important than any amount of fireworks it could generate. In fact, it caused her to look more shrewdly at the monster of her making.

She took a step closer.

Aside from a roughly humanoid form, there were few discernable features—no face, ears, forehead, or nose. Just piercing, red eyes staring out from a black pit.

Apollyon, demon of the Id.

If regret took a form, she imagined it would look something like this. But the closer she studied it, the more it seemed to be a patchwork of pieces. Stone-like fragments. A jigsaw of sediment. Assembled from shards of graphite or mineral.

Or crystal.

Crystal!

Suddenly, she remembered.

Eunice patted her thighs until she felt the lump in her right front pocket. She removed the onyx crystal and held it in her palm. "It's the last thing she gave me. She said it was… blessed."

Joseph stared. "It's an emblem. A physical token of her dissolution from reality. She's sorry. *Now* she's sorry. But you hold a piece. You took it!"

Eunice stared at the onyx crystal. Then she extended it to Joseph as if it were a hot potato.

"I don't want it," he protested. "It's a splinter from the gargoyle! It punctured your world." He stepped closer. "Regret—it crossed over. You shared it, nurtured it. *Now you're joined by it!* The bridge. That's the bridge you must complete."

She looked at the onyx crystal. Then she looked at the monster it had been carved from.

"I don't want it, either!" Eunice stared at the black glinting stone. "Never really did."

"Good!" Joseph steadied himself against the cyclone. "But you took it! You fed the engine. So give it back!"

"That's all?"

"Isn't that enough?"

She stared at the crystal and nodded. In the future, perhaps she could ponder the implications of such apparently minor concessions. But right now, unloading her personal regret was too inviting.

"You're going with me?" she said.

"You bet!"

She gripped the crystal, squeezing it as if to wring the rock of its poison. Taking a great breath, she plowed into the storm.

As they draw near, the loathsome black body grinded within itself. The vortex spun chaotically overhead, splashing red and orange refractions across the ground. Eunice fought the urge to look away from the monster. But she wanted this thing undone. *God, she wanted this over!* And if a stare-down was what it took, there was enough grief inside her to burn holes through a titanium tanker.

She may have yelled, shook her fists at the monstrosity. Nevertheless, she moved forward.

Because that was all you ever need to do.

Finally, they passed into the shadow of the onyx gargoyle. Eunice was dwarfed by the beast. It towered over them, flailing and snarling, radiating cool dark. Winterland reverberated with the creature's fury. But Eunice had crossed a line of terror into abandoned placidity. She stood in the eye of an emotional hurricane. So what if this monster could stomp her into oblivion. She was tired of carrying regret. *So very tired.*

There was only one thing left to do.

Eunice stood before the onyx gargoyle and extended the crystal.

"Take it back," she said. "We don't want it anymore."

The gargoyle bellowed. Its eyes grew into crimson slits and it bent forward. The harpies scattered, drawn up, up into the vortex, where they became little more than glowing embers fading in the night sky.

Eunice closed her eyes and grimaced as the creature snatched the crystal from her palm.

It was as if a Volkswagen had been removed from her body. How long had she been carrying this weight? Eunice collapsed. She was semi-conscious as Joseph slipped his arms underneath her and dragged her back, away from the contorting mass.

In some faraway place inside herself—perhaps a memory untainted by her own rot—she remembered her mother. Young. Vibrant. Full of life. Maybe places like that still existed in some distant corner of Winterland. If they did, perhaps such a place existed inside Eunice as well. She could only hope.

Eunice came to herself and sat up. Her eyes fixed on the onyx creature.

The gargoyle raised the glinting crystal before its bottomless face, as if admiring it. From deep within, a hole opened, a gash that seethed and expanded. The mouth was ringed with flaming teeth, like the hole in the sky. Vile sounds emerged, cackling and endless sobs. Air howled through the black vent.

Eunice scrambled to her feet and stood next to Joseph.

But the creature's red eyes rolled back up into its head.

The gargoyle's mouth grew. It was misshapen, not at all oval, and its edges ebbed, stretching wider and wider. Its eyes disappeared in the expanding orifice. And kept growing, swallowing everything. The creature was becoming a Mouth. Like a star against the night sky, the crystal danced before the tunnel that was a mouth, swinging in wide arcs as it had from Eunice's rear-view mirror, splashing light. Suddenly the crystal was plucked away and disappeared inside. The monster flailed, sucking its own limbs into the cavity with horrid, gulping sounds.

It was eating itself.

Didn't regret always do this?

Shrieks rose and the gale beat on them. Eunice staggered back, hands over her ears to stifle the cries. The onyx gargoyle grew smaller and smaller. Finally, the creature collapsed, folding in upon itself, leaving little more than an atmospheric smudge.

Little by little, the cyclone died. Dust and debris swirled to a stop across the highway. The fiery sky faded to a dusky pall. And Winterland grew still.

"Regret," Joseph mused, looking up into the halcyon twilight. "It's what held it all together."

Eunice stood, pensive, wondering what other monstrous emotions provided glue for interior worlds.

"The Coronation!" Joseph cried, scaring the tar out of her.

He gazed across the chasm.

Eunice traced the bridge with her eyes to a single throne. And her heart sank. Because she knew she was too late.

SIXTEEN

The moment her feet touched the bridge, she felt the first snowflake.

"It's her!" Eunice lunged forward. "Mother! I'm here!"

"Ain't made for bridges!" Mordant yelped.

The bridge swayed terribly as they ran, jostling them to no end. She dare not look into the abyss below her. Where it went and what other monsters it held, she could only imagine. Her oddball brigade trudged behind her, snorting, piping, and sniveling. Overhead, the silence continued—the soft, eerie quiet that snowfall brings. The red sky was gone, replaced by solemn gray.

"I tried to make it!" Her voice echoed in the chasm below. "I tried!"

The snow fell around her, obscuring her vision of the throne. Winterland was changing. Pockets of pristine glistening white gathered here and there.

Despite the exhaustion, Eunice ran, pushing herself forward across the bridge. She was crying, unsure whether it was from sadness or abject weariness. Finally, she stumbled off the bridge and collapsed. There was no time to wait for her party. Heaving herself off the ground, she brushed snow crystals from her eyes, and located the throne.

It was suspended in mid-air and looked like a large teardrop, jet-black, frozen between sky and earth. A solid obsidian droplet. Fear tore at her heart.

For the throne was empty.

"I'm too late!" Eunice ran and then crumbled helplessly to her knees before the throne. "No! I couldn't save her."

Joseph hurried to her side. Then Mordant, Ash, and Sybil encircled them, gaping at the empty throne. The snow swirled around them, a soft cool cocoon.

Even so, Joseph was laughing.

"Why?" Eunice shook her head. "Why bring me here for this?"

To most, her words would have seemed accusatory. But even a losing battle, if well fought, carried its own virtue. She suspected this was why Joseph was cracking up. She wanted to be offended at his brashness. However, leaving this throne vacant was probably a good reason to celebrate.

And now, Mordant, Ash and Sybil shuffled forward and stood before the empty throne like vassals to an invisible queen.

Eunice rose to her feet, swept the hair from her face and stared at them, for they were changing.

"Ain't fair!" Mordant cried, as his skin sloughed away from his frame. Black liquid seeped from his overalls and pooled at his feet. "Doomed! Mmmph! Drawn-n-quartered. All doomed!" he wailed, sinking ever lower into the slimy puddle. Soon, all that was left was his grubby clothes sopping in the tarry substance.

Reverend Ash swayed on his stilts, nose stuck high in the air in one last pious gesture. But his body had begun to fade. First his arms, then his legs. It was as if some atomic eraser was being passed over the venerable holy man, undoing him as it went.

"Here I stand," he warbled. "I can do no other."

Until he was completely gone. Only his stilts remained, teetering there by themselves, before they clattered to the ground before the throne.

Sybil was the last to go. Yet she was no longer a child. She hunched forward, now old and decrepit. Her skin had grayed.

"She loved us, Eunice." Sybil tried to giggle, but it was the gibberish of an old woman. "She loved us."

"I know," Eunice said. "She loved us too much to let us stay here."

Then Sybil's body wilted, turning skeletal, before dropping into a fleshy pile.

Eunice stood, staring blankly at what remained of her oddball crew: a black puddle, a rickety pair of stilts, and a bag of bones.

Homage to an empty throne.

The snow was falling hard. Eunice brushed tears from her cheeks. She turned to Joseph who was laughing with even more abandon. His hair was disheveled, speckled with white powder, and it appeared now more than ever, that his skull was dented, caved in on one side.

Exhaust fumes pelted her and she gasped.

"...hot... id... er..."

She steadied herself for the ground at her feet rippled. The warm, tingly curtain was nearby.

Joseph's eyes were bright, and there was a joyous timbre in his laughter. He had his head back, collecting snow crystals on his cheeks. She wanted to thank him and ask him more questions. But another sound pierced her brain.

The sirens had started again. The ghastly wail of the banshees.

No!

She doubled over, clamping her hands against her head, wincing until she squeezed water from her eyes.

"...ey'll... ee... in... utt..."

It was the Lexus man.

She opened her eyes enough to see concrete and lane lines, tainted dusky red. Another set of feet were near hers. The shrieks became sirens, rapidly approaching.

"It'll be all right..." the Lexus man had one hand on her back. She was bent over. "They're almost here."

Eunice straightened and looked around, at first frantically, and then with a sense of relief. Tears were on her cheeks and she brushed them aside. She was dizzy, braced herself against the man, and tried to re-orient. An ambulance cruised down the shoulder of the freeway, followed by a fire engine. The cry of Winterland was one with this world. Here and there, across the freeway, headlights awakened in the dusk.

"Where's Joseph?" Eunice asked, still trying to bridge the worlds.

"Who?"

"Joseph," she said. "The guy I hit."

"Lady," the Lexus man half-smiled, "you didn't hit anybody."

Everything returned to her. She patted the front of her jeans and the crystal was gone. Had it even been there at all?

"I need to sit down," she said, and did so on the spot.

The emergency vehicles pulled next to them on the shoulder. Someone shouted their way, something derogatory about women drivers. Red and yellow lights pulsated across the underbelly of the overpass. Two men came towards her from the ambulance, briskly, one with a black pouch.

"She's just dizzy, or something," the Lexus man said to them. "She's been... kinda lost. In shock I guess."

"C'mon!" It was the lady in the Lexus, chomping away, with her head out the window. "C'mon already. Geez!"

"They've gotcha now." He bent over, patted Eunice's back, nodded to the paramedics, and jogged to the other side of the Lexus where he got an earful from the driver.

Eunice leaned sideways, smiled and waved at him, mouthing the words, 'Thank you.'

The paramedics helped her up and got her car to the shoulder. They checked her blood pressure and pupils, asked some questions, and then give her a slip of paper that, she was sure, would translate into a hellacious bill.

She knew better than to tell them anything about Winterland.

By now, the sun had set. The smog was brown against orange. It appeared that miles of headlights were stacked behind them. Drivers were rubber-necking, angry eyes wanting to put a face on the last thirty minutes of stop and go.

While one of the paramedics finished the paperwork, the other watched her. But his gaze was not that of a man looking for a hot date. She made eye contact with him, and he looked away. His partner tossed the clipboard on the dash and climbed into the vehicle, waiting for his buddy to finish. Eunice and the paramedic stood together on the shoulder, awash in headlights.

"If you have any sensations of light-headedness again, pull over right away." He paused and she thought he wanted to say something else.

"Thank you. I will."

He nodded and turned towards the ambulance.

"Was there something else," she said. "Something you wanted to tell me?"

The paramedic turned to her. He was nervous, she could tell. "Go ahead," she coaxed. "What is it?"

After her excursion in Winterland, Eunice was ready for anything.

He cleared his throat. "This is the fourth time this year we've been to this same spot," he said. "Some of the guys say it's haunted." He tried to sound professional, but couldn't hide his humanity. "Same thing, every time: a guy ran in front of a car and got hit; traffic's backed up for miles. But no one was hit. No one was even there."

"Really?"

He squirmed. "Last year, some guy jumped off the overpass here, just a kid—killed himself."

They stood for a moment in what seemed reverent speechlessness.

A horn sounded and they both jumped. And laughed.

The paramedic shrugged. "Have a good evening, ma'am." He jogged back to the ambulance without looking back.

Eunice walked to the driver's side of her car, opened the door, and looked east. The sky was almost completely dark. Stars peeked through the veil of smog and a chain of wispy clouds with orange underbellies followed the foothills to the north. Hundreds of headlights shone her way. She stared into them and thought about Winterland, overlapping their world. Intersecting occasionally.

Then Eunice got in her Audi and drove to the hospital. She remained in the slow lane, for there was no need to hurry.

THE END

Mike Duran

DID YOU LIKE THIS BOOK?

If so, there's a couple ways you can help me and we can stay connected.

Without reviews, indie works like this one are almost impossible to market. Leaving a review will only take a minute—it doesn't have to be long or involved, just a sentence or two that tells people what you liked about this book, to help other readers know why they might like it, too, and to help me write more of what you might love. The truth is, VERY few readers leave reviews. Can you help me by being the exception? Thank you in advance!

I also have a mailing list. Signing up is simple (just your name and email addy). It's called *Mike Duran's Infrequent Updates* for a reason, as I promise not to clog your email with daily or weekly info. Signing up will keep you abreast of my new projects and give you opportunity to get discounts on some of my books and products. You can sign up for my mailing list at my website: www.mikeduran.com.

If you liked WINTERLAND, you may enjoy some of my other short fiction. WICKERS BOG is a tale of Southern Gothic Horror and SUBTERRANEA: NINE TALES OF DREAD AND WONDER, is an anthology of my short fiction that stylistically ranges from literary to pulp. Also available is my paranoir series which starts with THE GHOST BOX, a Publishers Weekly starred review item, followed in the series by SAINT DEATH: A Reagan Moon Novel. It is available in ebook or in print. CHRISTIAN HORROR: ON THE COMPATIBILITY OF A BIBLICAL WORLDVIEW AND THE HORROR GENRE is a non-fiction exploration of religious themes in horror, evangelical readers' objections to the genre, and a brief apologetic for the genre's compatibility with a biblical worldview. You can find links to some of my other articles, essays, and short stories at my website, as well as links to my other social media hangouts. That link is www.mikeduran.com. Once again, thanks so much for reading!

Mike Duran

Made in the USA
Middletown, DE
21 July 2018